THE BRIDGE

ALSO BY ANDREW PALMER

Awake

Whirlwind: Based on a True Story

Dark Frontier

Dark Frontier: The Awakening

THE BRIDGE

ANDREW PALMER

SYNAPZ PRODUCTIONS
TORONTO
WWW.SYNAPZPRODUCTIONS.COM

This story is based upon actual events, however, some of the characters and incidents portrayed and the names herein are fictitious, and any similarity to the name, character, or history of any person, living or dead, or any actual event is entirely coincidental and unintentional. Adapted from the screenplay by Andrew Palmer & Robyn Miller.

Book Design by Andrew Palmer.

ISBN-13: 979-8-776-93093-5

This book is dedicated to Big Tech
Actions have consequences.

Never doubt that a small group of thoughtful, committed citizens can change the world, indeed, it's the only thing that ever has.

-Margaret Mead

CHAPTER 1

The sounds of the river and the birds, the wind and the crickets, all seemed to fade into the background over time, but the clang of hammers and anvils never did, even in the still of the afternoons. While the animals took shelter from the hot sun, the workers laboured on.

Calls split the air and the man at a coal furnace straightened up briefly to look at the structure spanning the river. Behind a thick, canvas apron and long work gloves, his skin rippled with corded muscle, holding a sheen of sweat and a liberal coating of grime.

Without taking his eyes from the structure, he pulled one hand out of a glove and wiped his brow quickly. Blue eyes, far from unusual amongst the Quebecoise workers, stood out startling and clear against soot-streaked skin.

A huge team was accompanying a section of the bridge as it was moved into place to be lifted. Horses strained and men hooked the carrying cables around it. This was as much an art as a science, hard-won lessons in safety mixing with an intuition of which cable might be a bit weak, which specific place on the beam might be best for the cable. The men shouted to one another without looking up, the language of the jobsite and their familiarity with one another helping them move as one unit.

The man at the furnace slid his hand back into the glove and rotated one shoulder with a wince before reaching into the furnace with tongs. Amongst the flames, rivets were heating, and he selected one of just the right shade.

He cast a glance over his shoulder before tossing the glowing rivet through the air. It whistled in a neat arc before it was snatched out of the air by a Catcher with an expert maneuver of an ash-lined leather bucket. The boy flashed a smile before turning to hold the bucket out to a Holder-on, who set the rivet in place on one of the steel beams.

As the Holder-on steadied the rivet, another man gave it several heavy strikes with a hammer, flattening it permanently in place.

By the time the head of the rivet was flattened, the whole operation was beginning again, another rivet already in the air. There was no time for rest at this worksite—or for rubbernecking, no matter how impressive the feats as men hauled great pieces of steel skyward.

On a hill overlooking both the river and the site, a large man stood with his hands in the pockets of his suit pants. His eyes were fixed on the bridge, and there was a frown on his face. He shifted slowly but continuously: crossing his arms, then putting his hands back in his pockets, shifting his weight.

The man with the hammer wiped at his brow with one sleeve and took a sip of water from a nearby jug before looking up. He frowned as well when he saw the man in the suit, and waited for the other to look at him.

When the man in the suit cocked his head in a silent question, the Hammerer looked around the worksite. Evidently reassured by what he saw, he gave a nod back to the man in the suit, who relaxed slightly. He wandered away in a slow circle, watching his shoes, lost in thought.

Behind him, a temporary building served as the office for the construction site. Inside lay piles of documents and sketches that never could be kept neat—this wasn't some city office, after all, but one on an active site, where any set of schematics might need to be pulled out at any time.

The clop of a horse's hooves sounded, and a whistle split the air.

The suited man looked up to see a young telegram boy on horseback, both horse and rider sweaty from the trip.

"Can I help you?" The man cleared his throat; between the dust and the heat, it was dry.

The boy held up an envelope. "I have a telegram for the site engineer."

"That's me." The man strode over to take the telegram, and, as he tore it open, looked over to where the beam was now being lifted.

The groan began so slowly that it seemed to come from inside the bones of those present. Men began to turn and look before they knew what they were looking at, and the site engineer -scanning the telegram- lifted his head like a deer listening for footsteps. The horse pranced nervously, and the boy reined it in sharply.

There was a pause while the world seemed to hang in complete stillness…and then the groan rose to a metallic screech, accompanied by the indrawn, horrified breath of every man on site. The site engineer burst into motion and sprinted for the slope, but even as he was moving, so was the bridge: sliding, twisting, toppling—

B en leaned forward and rubbed at his eyes. He had a headache developing at his right temple, and his stomach wasn't feeling too good. Skipping breakfast had been a mistake.

Staying up until 2:30AM, drinking expired beer, probably hadn't been the greatest idea either—but, hey, it was his senior spring. He had a few good leads on jobs, he didn't have any tough classes this semester, and the weather had been fantastic. He figured he might as well take full advantage of the freedoms of university life while he still had the opportunity to do so.

Up at the front of the classroom, Professor McLeary had switched to a black and white photograph of a man with a heavy moustache and round, wire-rimmed glasses.

"Rudyard Kipling," McLeary told the class, "had referred to engineers in some of his earlier poems and stories, which is why the Institute felt he would be the ideal person to fashion a ritual for the Iron Ring ceremony."

Ben wondered if Kipling had known that his work would one day be used to inflict a slow death by boredom on engineering students. He rubbed at his face again and considered putting it down on the cool surface of the desk.

"Hey." Tyler gave a hiss and nudged him with an elbow. "I'm about to come up on that corner again." His fingers were flying over the keys of his laptop, but he wasn't taking notes. Instead, he was guiding a pixelated car through a crowded city, running lights and avoiding pedestrians by a hairsbreadth.

That was, when he *did* miss them. It seemed to be a 50% chance of whether or not he tried at all, and his eyes kept straying to the timer in the upper right-hand corner of the screen.

Ben eyed a few of the stats. "You're going to have the po after you if you keep hitting people."

"If I keep going around them, I'm not going to beat your time," Tyler shot back, not looking up from the screen.

There was a hiss from a few rows ahead of them and both boys looked up to see a girl with short, black hair, glaring at them. Esther Emami was one of the top students in their year, and she had a definite reputation…as a robot. She'd been here all four years, but Ben had yet to see her at a party.

Sorry, Ben mouthed.

She sighed and turned back to her notes.

"—Based on one of his poems," Professor McLeary was saying, "called 'The Sons of Martha.' It refers to the engineers who toil without end, in order to make the world function smoothly, while their counterpart, the 'Sons of Mary,' enjoy the fruits of their labour."

"So, why are we trying to be the Sons of Martha?" Ben asked Tyler in a whisper, with a frown. "That sounds like a bad deal."

"Huh?" Tyler didn't look over. "Almost there, almost—*dammit*!" As he tried to get around a hairpin turn, his car spun out against a side wall, and was now shown in stylized pieces with his character standing, incongruously, in the middle of a cloud of pixelated smoke.

Ben guffawed.

There was a sudden silence in the room, and most people turned to look at the two of them.

Professor McLeary blinked rather owlishly. "What was that, Mr. O'Betany?"

Ben wished he could sink through the floor. Tyler was smirking at him, and Esther seemed torn between being glad that he'd finally gotten caught, and annoyed that he'd managed to interrupt the lecture again.

"Sorry," Ben said. "I was, uh—sorry." He looked at the professor. "Nothing to add, professor."

"Mmm." The man nodded and turned back to the screen. "Where was I? Yes. Rooted in Luke, Chapter 10 of the Bible, the parable of Martha and Mary. That's all for today, please read Chapter 23 for our next class. I will also be giving you details on your final projects, so make sure not to skip—"

Ben had already tuned out. As soon as the lights came on, he shoved his books into his backpack and jiggled it a little to make them sink down through the morass of crumpled assignments and old chip bags. Around them, students were talking and taking their time leaving; this was the last class of the day and, with the school year winding down, the classroom full of seniors was taking things easy.

"Come on." Ben kicked at Tyler's foot while he zipped up his backpack and turned back to his own laptop.

"Dude, wait." Tyler snapped his fingers to get Ben's attention. "Check it out. The Redsuits are throwing a backyard keg party!"

Ben leaned over to see a party invitation. A group of engineering students in red jumpsuits, decorated with a flare, along with a couple of photos of a backyard, some Jell-O shots, and assorted hints of debauchery. The gallery of photos came with a post inviting junior and senior engineering students to a backyard keg party to celebrate the end of the semester.

The Redsuits were notorious on campus. As the official Welcome Week team for first-years, they were made up of students from all subcategories in the engineering program at McMaster. While they were, unsurprisingly, some of the highest-achieving students, their numbers also included some of the top partiers of the department, who seemed to approach "work hard, play hard" as a mantra.

There was a house on Sterling Street where at least a few of the Redsuits lived every year. Their parties were legendary, and Ben had no idea how some of them managed to do so well in school after the late nights they regularly pulled.

"It's going to be *epic*," Tyler said, drawing out the last word. "Like *half* of them are graduating, or something, so they're going out with a bang. Matt said that there's gonna be some pub crawl thing, but

instead of bars, we hit all the houses on that block?
And—during finals. This is like the warmup."

"Right." Ben grinned. "Well, if they're going to
warm up before the main event, we should, too." He
and Tyler might not be Redsuits, but they'd made
enough friends amongst the group that they were
invited to all the parties—and Tyler was right, this
was exactly the year to go out with a bang. Then he
stopped. "Wait, but…"

"What?" Tyler closed his laptop and slid it into his
bag.

"Our Materials assignment." Ben tipped his head
back and groaned. "It's due tomorrow and I haven't
even started it. Have you?"

"Nope." Tyler snorted to show what he thought of
that idea. "Anyway, who cares? We'll do what we did
last time." He gave a meaningful nod at Esther.

Ben swallowed.

"What?" Tyler gave him a look. "Come on.
What?"

"Last time was supposed to *be* the last time." Ben
leaned over to speak more quietly. "And we nearly
got caught because you didn't change it enough.
Remember?"

"So, I'll change it more this time." Tyler didn't
bother dropping his voice. He looked over and rolled
his eyes when he saw that Ben was still hesitating.
"Jesus, stop being a little bitch and hurry up. They tap
the kegs at five and I gotta shower." He nodded again
at the girl in front of them, and finally dropped his
voice. "And she's getting ready to leave."

Ben squeezed his eyes shut for a moment, but he
had already made his decision. He shook his head and

opened the command screen on his laptop with a few well-practiced keystrokes. His fingers were a blur until he hit *enter* emphatically, and a moment later, Esther's desktop showed up on his screen, mirrored from where her laptop was still open a few rows down from them.

Her desktop background was a picture of Esther with a dog—or, rather, Esther nearly hidden by gigantic dog, grey-haired and shaggy, that was sitting in her lap. The picture was superimposed on a pink background decorated with flowing typography: *"The most difficult thing is the decision to act, the rest is merely tenacity. -Amelia Earhart."*

Ben opened up her documents folder. He knew the file path to follow from the last time he had hacked Esther's computer, but he was struck all over again by the exquisitely well-organized filing system. Her Materials assignment was hanging out in the neatly organized documents folder, under Assignments, Engineering, Senior Year, Spring, and Materials. Ben grabbed it and noticed that the document hadn't been opened for days. When he checked, however, the assignment was fully done.

Apparently, she had finished it with a minimum of fuss. Ben shook his head. He was impressed despite himself.

"Damn," he muttered to himself.

"What?" Tyler was jiggling one foot impatiently.

"This girl is *smart*." Ben gestured at the assignment. "How'd she finish this so fast?"

Tyler reached out to press Ben's laptop closed. "She probably has no life."

Ben had a hard time disagreeing with that, so he shrugged.

"Is that it?" Tyler drummed his fingers on the desk.

"Right. Yeah." Ben shook himself and looked away from where Esther was now packing up her pens, notebooks, and laptop.

"Sweet. Let's go." Tyler was already halfway to the stairs. "If we're gonna pregame, we gotta move."

Ben laughed as he followed.

An hour and a couple of shots later, the two of them were squeezing their way into 100 Sterling Street, a rental property lovingly referred to by its tenants as, 'The Century Club'. It was once a lovely, brick house in a posh neighbourhood, but the property owners had since given up trying to clean it fully between each group of university students. The lease on this particular house was passed down each year to the leading member of the Redsuits, though Ben didn't have the first idea how they managed to get the landlord to renew. The walls were pockmarked with everything from nail holes, of old pictures, to larger holes that looked like they might be from hammers or fists.

Out on the patio in the back, a group was cheering an intense game of flip cup, between a first-year and a senior. The first-year was tall and broad-shouldered—a starter on the football team, if Ben remembered correctly—but he couldn't yet match the skill *or* alcohol tolerance of his opponent. He was currently ahead, but it wasn't looking good for him.

On a stage in the corner, some of the BioMed seniors were giving an impromptu performance, rocking out on guitars and drums while students formed a mosh pit in front of the stage.

Tyler grabbed a beer for Ben and the two clinked rims before draining the cups in one long gulp.

"*Woof.*" Ben grimaced. "They didn't spend much on beer, I see."

"You're doing it all wrong." Tyler shook his head. "If you drink fast enough, you don't taste it. Shots?" He disappeared toward the house without waiting for an answer.

Ben was grinning when his phone buzzed. He pulled it out of his pocket, saw MOM on the screen, and declined the call with a sigh. She was calling to check up on plans for after graduation—and he had precisely zero intention of discussing that at a party. His mother was going to be earnest and tell him all about how he really *should* be sending in more applications, no matter whether Ben lied to her or not about how many he sent.

He had *intended* to send in a few. He had most of his materials together. That had to count for something. And he'd start working on it soon. He knew he had to; the last thing he wanted to do was hear his mother get all intense about it.

Someone stumbled drunkenly into Ben and he reached out a hand automatically to catch them. It was a girl, her brown hair falling loose around her shoulders. She gave an embarrassed laugh. "Sorry."

"Falling for me already?" Ben raised an eyebrow at her. He'd seen one of the Redsuits use that line a few weeks ago, and he'd practiced it in his room a few times since then…like a total nerd.

But whether it was the beer or the practice, the girl giggled. She sipped at her own beer and looked up at Ben through her lashes.

"Hey." Tyler was back with shots, and he gave a grin as he came up beside Ben. "Who's the cutie, Ben?"

"We haven't been introduced yet." Ben smiled at her. "So, what's—"

The crowd behind them moved suddenly, and someone jostled Tyler forward. One of the shots, dyed bright blue, splashed across the girl's shirt.

She gave a hiss and brushed at the liquid, which was already seeping into the shirt. "*Seriously*?" she demanded, and stalked off.

Tyler winced and watched her go before presenting Ben with the empty shot glass. "Sorry, man," he said solemnly. "I guess you…lost your shot."

"Ugh." Ben groaned. "No puns. Please, no puns."

"More drinks, then!" Tyler downed his own shot. "Come on, let's get you one."

CHAPTER 3

Ben had gone out of his way to get a ringtone for his phone that sounded like an old-school landline. It had seemed like a neat thing at the time but was not nearly so cute this morning. The sound felt like it had wormed its way between the plates of his skull and just set up shop, vibrating like a tiny set of jackhammers.

Ben picked up his head and groaned. His neck ached. Apparently, he had just fallen asleep in one of the chairs near the TV, while Tyler had passed out on the couch. The TV was still showing a loading screen for Mario Kart, bright enough that it made Ben wince.

"Mmf." Tyler turned over on the couch. "Jesus, make that thing stop."

"Right." Ben felt around in his pockets, and then down amidst the couch cushions—in doing so, he managed to accidentally accept the call.

As he fumbled for the phone, a man's voice came out of the speaker, and Ben pressed it up to his ear eagerly. "Dad?" At the response, though, his shoulders slumped. "Oh. Yeah. Hi, Steve. Yeah, I'm fine. You? Sure. Good to hear. I really have to—" There were more words from the other end of the line and he tried to hold back a sigh. "Yeah, I'll talk to her." Ben rubbed at the back of his neck, where tension was already accumulating.

Tyler sat up with a grimace, clutching one side of his head.

"Hi, Mom," Ben replied, after a bright hello from the other end of the line.

In the corner of his field of vision, Tyler groped for one of the drawers next to the couch. He fished around and triumphantly pulled out a Ziploc bag with a few pre-rolled joints in it.

"Yeah, I have enough food." Ben passed a hand over his eyes. "Yes. Mom, I'm on the meal plan. Yeah. Yeah. No. Look, Mom—I gotta go. Okay, love you, too. Bye." He ended the call and dropped it onto the chair next to him with a groan.

"And how is Mommy Dearest?" Tyler asked as he lit the joint. He took a long drag and passed it to Ben.

"Exactly how you think she is." Ben took the joint. His head was pounding, and his stomach—which had never quite stopped being queasy yesterday—was worse this morning.

"Good old Tracy." Tyler held out a hand and twitched his fingers for the joint. After his next drag, he held his breath for a long moment before letting it out slowly. "Could be a lot worse."

Ben felt a squirm of guilt. He looked over to see Tyler staring out the window and knew he had messed up. Neither Tyler nor Ben ever missed an opportunity to make fun of Ben's mother, with her constant calls and her endless worrying, but—

"At least your mother calls you," Tyler said bitterly.

"I know I shouldn't complain," Ben said. His head was too cloudy to figure out how to say the right thing right now. "I just—"

Tyler waved his hand and avoided the conversation by standing up and heading into his bedroom.

Ben grimaced and tried to figure out if he had time to shower. First, he should see if he needed to—

Yeah, he *definitely* needed to shower. He looked around at the mess to see if he had left his toiletry bag within reach. He didn't see it immediately, but that wasn't necessarily a sign that it wasn't here. The common room between the two bedrooms, after all, was pretty much what he assumed his mother's worst nightmare would be. Every once in a while, she visited and presented him with yet another custom-made, "cleaning made simple" plan, after which she took four hours of his day showing him how to dust things and get various stains out of clothing.

The common room, as a counterpoint, was filled with pop cans, sticky red plastic cups, dirty clothes, and old pizza boxes. There were piles of schoolwork and engineering textbooks in several places— including under the utilitarian, grey couch—and some half-finished cups of coffee that had probably grown mold by now.

Tyler came back from his room with two cold beers from his mini-fridge and held one out to Ben. "Hair of the dog?"

Ben reached for it, then grimaced. "We've got class in like half an hour."

"Dude." Tyler nodded to where the sun was filtering down through the leaves of the trees outside the window.

Between the branches, Ben could see bright blue sky. He looked back at Tyler with a raised eyebrow. "What?"

"Look at the *weather*, Let's just take the day and go to Webster Falls, right?" Tyler sighed at the look on Ben's face. "*What*?"

"It's almost crunch time," Ben told him miserably. "No, seriously. And finals are—"

"All right, all right, don't get your panties in a bunch." Tyler rolled his eyes and stubbed out the joint.

"We should, uh—" Ben stood up and regretted it when the room spun. If he sat back down, though, he was definitely not getting to class. He looked around. "I'm gonna take a quick shower."

"Suit yourself." Tyler sat down and picked the joint back up.

A shower helped Ben feel more human, but he was still spaced out through the rest of the day. By the time the two of them reached Ethics, Ben was seriously doubting his ability to make life choices. The joint he finished with Tyler—between the last two classes of the day—had helped with his nausea, but he was still feeling far from one hundred percent. He sat in the back of the class and tried to just make it through the presentation, mostly zoning out while Professor McLeary droned on about the Iron Ring ceremony, and Tyler scrolled through pictures of the previous night's party.

At one point, Tyler chuckled and turned his laptop for Ben to see it. "Hey, look. Dude. Look."

Ben made a complaining noise and opened one eye, then leaned forward to see a group of girls. He wasn't sure what he was looking for until Tyler pointed to one in particular, who was doing her best to hide the blue stain on her shirt.

"You got her gooooood," Tyler said, drawing out the last word on a high note.

"*You* got her," Ben corrected him. "I was just the innocent bystander whose play you ruined."

"Uh-huh." Tyler chuckled and went back to scrolling. "Gotta be able to pivot, man. A new one comes along every little while."

Ben sighed and laid his head back on the wall, but not before seeing Esther—this time sitting several rows in front of them—giving the two of them an annoyed glare. He didn't have the energy to mouth another apology at her today, so he just sat back and yawned, then continued watching the presentation through slitted eyes.

"Therefore," McLeary said, switching to a slide that showed a dented and rough-hewn ring, "the Iron Ring was created as a symbol and daily reminder of the ethical obligation that engineers take during the Ritual Calling ceremony."

Esther raised her hand.

Professor McLeary looked over. "Yes, Esther?"

"What happens in the ceremony?" Esther asked him. Her pen was poised for more notes.

Professor McLeary, however, only smiled enigmatically. "Ahh, well—you'll have to be invited to find out."

Esther frowned slightly.

"The ceremony is kept very private," Professor McLeary explained. "In earlier generations, only graduates and other established engineers were allowed to witness it. Now, family members are allowed to watch the ceremony, but we still make a habit not to speak of it to those who were not present, either as a graduate, or to honour one."

Esther nodded seriously.

"Now," Professor McLeary to all of them. "As I mentioned at the start of the last class, the topic for your final assignment will be, 'What the Iron Ring Means to Me.'"

Ben couldn't help but smile. An opinion essay? This was going to be easy. Beside him, he heard Tyler snort, and the two boys shared a grin.

"What I did not say the other day, however," McLeary continued, "is that you will be partnered up for this project. I have found that ethical *discussions* tend to be much deeper than ethical…monologues, as it were. I have also found that these discussions are more fruitful when the teams are chosen for you, so I have partnered you all up at random. I have the list here at the front of the room, and will also post it on my faculty page later today. Dismissed."

"Let's go see who we got." Ben crossed his fingers.

"I'll check." Tyler stood up hurriedly and went down the stairs, leaving Ben staring after him bemusedly. He pushed through the crowd to look, and sprinted back up with a grin that made Ben deeply uneasy.

"What?" Ben asked, as Tyler came up the stairs.

"You got *Esther*," Tyler said in a sing-song voice. "Enjoy your slow death, dude. Or—I'm going to offer again—bunk off and come to Webster Falls with me for the rest of the day."

Ben raised an eyebrow. "And who did *you* get?"

Tyler waved a hand. "Come on, let's go."

"Nah, I should do some studying."

"Oh, well, in *that* case…incoming." Tyler headed out with a wide, insincere smile at Esther, who had come up the stairs behind him.

"Uh…" Ben stared at Esther. "I hear we're partners?"

"Yeah." She didn't look pleased. "And we need to talk about—are you *high*?"

Ben cleared his throat. "It's, uh…medicinal."

Esther took a deep breath, as if for patience.

"So, what about the assignment?" Ben wanted to get through this discussion sooner rather than later. He was craving a pizza, a beer, and a nap, in any order.

I'm not going to have you sink my grade in this class."

"Okay." Ben nodded with as much enthusiasm as he could muster. "Got it."

"I'm *serious*." She was looking more annoyed by the second. "Don't you ever pay attention to what matters?"

"Yeah, I do, actually." Ben put his laptop back in his backpack and stood. "But this is basically an elective course, and the project is a gimme, let's be real."

She gave him a look that could have peeled paint. "I know you don't care about your grades," she told him precisely, "but I do, and I am not carrying you for this assignment. Meet me in Thode tomorrow for research." She wheeled around and headed back to the stairs, but stopped when she got there to pin him with a look. "And, Ben?"

"Yeah."

"Be ready to work."

"Work? Research? It's an *opinion* question." But she was gone. Ben sighed and loaded up his backpack. This sounded like it had about a snowball's chance in hell of being anything other than a shitshow.

CHAPTER 4

Esther hurried past several student houses. The brick exteriors had charmed her when she was little. She had imagined that they were filled with students sitting at desks, earnestly focusing on mathematics and science, engineering, business…

She now knew that what happened in those houses was not often related to studying.

Or…

Her footsteps slowed and she looked at one of the houses. A boy and a girl were standing on the steps, clearly flirting. The girl was playing with the strap of her backpack, and the boy was pretending to lounge against the door, as if he was completely at ease. Everything about them seemed unusually clear, from the weave of the girl's jeans to the soft sweep of the boy's black hair across his forehead.

She felt the familiar twinge of annoyance. This wasn't schoolwork, and she could be damned near certain that their evening plans included red plastic cups, frozen pizzas, and drinking games. Esther had come here to be somebody, to finally earn her place somewhere. Engineers did important work and she had imagined them as a close-knit society, bound together by shared values and hard work.

And then she had gotten here, and it seemed like none of them even cared.

"Hey." The boy's voice jolted her out of her reverie. "You lost or something?"

Esther flushed. "Yeah. Sorry. Just...end of semester stuff, I guess."

To her surprise, both of them laughed.

"I feel you," the boy said. He flashed a smile her way. "You're in my Materials class, right? This week's assignment is killer."

Esther hadn't had a problem with it, but she knew better than to say that. She smiled and hoisted her backpack—then, not sure what to say, she gave an awkward wave and hurried away, putting her headphones in her ears.

Slowly, her anxiety faded away and her equilibrium returned.

Esther's parents kept offering to help her buy a used car, saying that she would need it as soon as she was working full time, but Esther had so far refused. The walks to and from school, listening to all different kinds of music, were one of the only times she could get her brain to "turn off." At any other time, there was something she should be doing—but, when she was walking, she could allow herself to relax.

Today, she was listening to a playlist she had made when she was 13, and some of the songs had held up remarkably well. She was still humming along when she got home and put away her headphones, slipping off her shoes and putting them on the rack inside the door.

The Emami home was modest, one of the smaller houses in its neighbourhood. The walls were covered in family photographs, many from Esther's paternal family in Tabriz, and her maternal family in Tehran. Both her mother and father felt a deep connection to the homeland they had left long ago, even as they realized that they likely would not have met if they had not come to Canada.

In the front room, Esther's father sat with his mother, Marjane, both watching a soccer match. The roar of the crowd filtered through, and Esther smiled slightly while she went to check the score.

"We came back strong after half-time," her father told her. "We'll win this."

Esther smiled fondly. Her father was endlessly hopeful about his favorite football team—which, for reasons she had never understood, was Olympique de Marseille, instead of any of the football clubs from Tabriz, or even the rest of Iran. Whether they were on a winning streak or a losing streak, whether the game had been good or bad, no matter how many minutes there were left to go, Anoosh would be utterly certain that his team was going to win.

Right now, with the game tied at the 78th minute, Esther figured that the chances of a win were better than usual. Anoosh had set the old PVR to record each game, and he avoided all sports news until he had watched them in order; and so the rest of the family had gradually adopted the same strategy, which was fairly easy when the football club in question was in France instead of Canada.

Her father gave a cheer and jumped out of his seat, only to press a hand over his heart in exaggerated sadness. "Oh, that was *beautiful*! So close to going in. Next time."

Even though the ball had not gone into the net, he held up his hand for a high five, and Marjane pressed her shaking hand against his. At ninety years old, she had lost the ability to speak, but was still smiling, enjoying both the soccer game and her son's investment in it.

Esther padded into the kitchen to find her mother cooking, the scents of greens and fruits heavy in the air.

"Hello, Mama." Esther kissed her mother on the cheek and went to get a glass of water. "How much time until dinner? I was going to study—"

"Dinner is almost ready." Fareen fixed Esther with a glare and nodded to the kitchen table. "Sit. Tell me about your day."

Esther sighed. Family time was non-negotiable in this household, and she sometimes resented it. It wasn't that she objected to spending time with her family—even her younger sister, Yasmine, who was going through a particularly infuriating phase right now—it was just that Esther wanted, sometimes, to have time that was just *hers*. She wanted to set her own priorities.

It wasn't like she was asking very much, either, she thought. She just wanted to be able to take her dinner up to her room with her and eat while she studied. She wanted to be able to make her own choices, to have the tiniest bit of space to decide which priorities she wanted to have.

It wasn't like she was trying to avoid ever talking to her family again. She just wanted them to respect her.

"Esther?" her mother prompted.

"Sorry. Um." She thought back. "I found out who my partner is for the Ethics assignment. That's the one I mentioned about the Iron Ring."

"Who is it?" Her mother did not look over from where her cleaver was flashing, chopping whole bunches of greens together.

"You don't know him. His name is Ben." Esther sighed and sat back.

Her mother looked over. "That wasn't a happy sigh."

"He doesn't take anything seriously," Esther explained. "Or—sometimes he seems like he does, and then he goes back to treating school like this huge joke. It's such a waste."

"You sound twice your age and with teenagers of your own," her mother said fondly. "Esther, I know we're strict with you sometimes—"

"Sometimes?" Esther joked.

Her mother gave her a look that was equal parts exasperated and amused. "This doesn't hold a candle to your father's life and mine, growing up in Iran."

"Yes, you've said."

"You don't remember some of the fights your Baba and I had with *his* mother." Fareen had lowered her voice. "She told us that you and Yasmine would grow up with no respect, no character. She thought we were coddling you."

"Really?" Esther could hardly imagine that. Marjane could not speak any longer, of course, but her silence usually held a smile. She seemed quite pleased with the world.

"She can't argue with how you two turned out," Fareen said with a smile. "But sometimes I think you might be a bit *too* serious when it comes to schoolwork, Esther. Having your life be all one thing isn't good for you. Your Baba found a good living in business, and he could still find you a job if—"

"Mama, please." This argument had been ongoing for years, and Esther had long ago given up hope that her parents would stop trying to get her to switch majors. However, with graduation now so close she could almost taste it, the familiar conversation made her want to scream.

"You need balance," her mother said, unperturbed by Esther's tone. "Maybe this boy will be good for you."

"You wouldn't be happy if I started behaving like Ben," Esther told her flatly. "He was high in class today."

Her mother pursed her lips and shook her head. "No, I wouldn't approve of that, you're right. But perhaps…perhaps you two will learn from one another, hmm?"

"Not much time for that. The semester's over in a few days and we'll be off to our jobs." Esther shrugged. "And I can't afford to let up. Any of the places that will help me pay for a Masters will want evidence that I can buckle down and work."

She stood up and started taking out silverware. Setting the table was Yasmine's job, but the sound of her sister's voice, laughing and talking loudly, led Esther to believe that Yasmine probably wouldn't get to the task before dinner was ready—plus, it might make her mother more likely to let her take a plate upstairs.

She set out the utensils and dishes, made sure there were trivets in place on the table, and filled water glasses before coming back to the kitchen to sit.

Fareen, uncharacteristically, did not comment on Esther's plans for graduate school. She put food onto serving plates and handed them to Esther one by one for her to put on the table. When she was done, the cooking pots and pans went into the sink and Fareen gave Esther a kiss on the forehead.

"It's a mother's job to make sure she drives her teenager absolutely crazy," she told Esther.

"Mom, I'm 22."

"So, you see, I'm doing well." Her mother smiled. "Yasmine! Dinner!"

"*Coming!*" was the response, and Yasmine appeared not too long after, rolling her eyes. "Sorry, I was trying to talk with Jamie, but this boy kept calling. He literally can't take no for an answer."

"Block his calls," Esther said tersely.

"I told you, I was talking to Jamie."

"If he kept interrupting you, wouldn't it make more sense to—"

Yasmine cut her off. "Plus, I don't have time. I need to work on more practice sessions tonight. "I got such a good response from the last one. I just need to do my warm-ups. It's a lot of pressure when it's live."

Esther only barely refrained from rolling her eyes. Despite Yasmine's insistence that she was going to be a singer, Esther seemed to be the one their parents worried about. Yasmine, of course, was still only 17, but Esther was beginning to worry about her sister's chances of getting into a good university.

"Girls." Fareen's voice cut through the chatter. "You're holding up everyone from having their dinner. Go out to the table, please."

"I'll be eating in my room," Esther said.

Her mother looked back sharply from the dining room. "You will not. Dinner is family time."

"I have a ton of studying to do." Esther came out and grabbed a plate, serving herself some rice and chicken stew, as well as cheese and flatbread. The family had their non-Iranian favorites, such as pizza, but most meals were the foods Fareen and Anoosh had grown up with.

"Esther Emami, you sit down right now." Her mother's voice was stern.

Something inside Esther snapped. "Ground me if you want, Mom, but I need to get started. It's crunch time for the semester."

"She's so dramatic," Yasmine said in a stage whisper as Esther left.

Esther sighed and kept walking. She heard her parents talking and the clink of serving spoons as she went up the stairs. In her room, she set her dinner plate down on the desk and realized she had forgotten her backpack downstairs.

Her Materials book was here, at least. She could start by studying for that final. Esther flipped open the book and sat down. She was already relaxing now that she was in her own space. Her room wasn't large, but it was *hers*. She had covered the walls with movie posters, with her favorite—Jurassic Park—taking pride of place above her bed.

She put her earbuds in and began to work, sinking into the familiar reverie. When she got done with school, she told herself, it would be different. The people who made it in engineering would be devoted and hard-working. She had never found her niche here, but things would change soon.

They would. They *would*.

CHAPTER 5

Thode Library was the sort of space that was caught between eras. Colourful murals had been thrown up on some of the walls and there was open space devoted to experimentation and studying, with a few models set up. Right now, some frosh were looking deeply tired and overwhelmed by their first spring, clustered around a table as they tried to hide their travel mugs full of coffee.

Ben smiled slightly. *Everyone* got panicked around this time of year, no matter how far they were through their degree or how much they studied during the rest of the school year, but first-years always had a particularly anxious look to them.

It seemed like just yesterday that he'd been one of them. He'd still had a ridiculous haircut at that point, and was in the middle of a disastrous attempt to grow a beard. He had also been completely panicked that partying had sunk his GPA so much that he might flunk out.

It had taken him a while to unwind once he got here. Tyler seemed to have been born with the skill. He lived university the same way he had lived high school: never quite the linchpin of the party, but always there, always up for a good time. Ben would have been a hopeless square if Tyler hadn't been around to drag him out to parties and get him out of his own head.

A square like...Esther, who was probably waiting for him. Ben grimaced and turned for the stairs. Behind him, there was the angry blare of the scanner, as someone tried to leave with a book they hadn't checked out. Probably a genuine mistake, Ben figured. He had worked in the library during first and second year, before his father had come through with an allowance so that he wouldn't have to spend 15 hours per week paying the bills.

Panicked, sleep-deprived students tended to pass-out right on their desks in the study rooms, and they *definitely* tended to leave without checking-out books.

Down in the old stacks, Ben walked past the row of empty tables, and around the back of the long room. He was halfway through a set of pictures from a recent party when his phone stalled out and he held it up to try to get a signal, tapping at it in frustration.

"You might as well turn it off," Esther said. "They're running maintenance on the Wi-Fi this morning."

"That sucks." Ben pocketed his phone. "How are we supposed to research anything, then?"

Esther reached over to a stack of books next to her and tapped them, annoyed. "The old-fashioned way. Have you ever used the library?"

"Actually, I used to work here." Ben sat down in his seat, swinging his backpack off his shoulders, and looked her in the eyes. "So..."

To his surprise, she sighed and rubbed at her forehead. "I'm sorry. It...hasn't been a great day so far."

"It's only 11AM," Ben said blankly. "How much can have gone wrong already?"

She just shook her head out and pulled out a notebook, flipping through notes that showed sketches of bridge construction, and writing in both English and—

"Arabic?" Ben said.

"Farsi," Esther said. When Ben frowned, she sighed. "Same alphabet—now—but different language. My family's from Iran, so I'm not Arab."

"Sure." Ben nodded and hoped he didn't look as lost as he felt.

She could tell he was, though. "Iran is Persian," she said. "It's a whole thing. There were caliphates and invasions and—yeah. Complicated. But we're not Arab, and that's not Arabic."

Ben put his backpack on a nearby table and sat, pulling out his own notebook. "Sounds like you've given that speech more than once."

"Yep." She gave him a look. "It happens often enough that sometimes I just don't have the energy to talk about it again and sometimes..." She shook her head. "Sometimes I start caring again." She looked over at him. "Just—please don't ask me if I've got an arranged marriage set up or why I'm not wearing a headscarf, okay? I do *not* have the energy for that right now."

Ben gave a thumbs-up. "So, what happened this morning?"

"What? Oh." She sighed and pulled her hair back from her face. "My mom wanted to pick a fight. I didn't have dinner with everyone last night and…probably not important."

"Everyone?" Ben asked.

"My parents, my sister. My Mama—ah, grandmother. My dad's mother. Family dinner is a big deal for my parents." She rolled her eyes, looking embarrassed.

"Doesn't sound so bad," Ben said, before he could help himself.

"No?" She raised an eyebrow. "You don't think it sounds super lame?"

"I didn't say *that*." Ben held up a finger, lips twitching. "I just said it didn't sound so *bad*. My dinner last night was…uh…actually, I don't know if I ate anything. Wait, yes I did. Chips. With Tyler." He shrugged. "It's kind of sweet that your whole family eats together, right?"

"Right." Esther sighed again. "Look, I'm not…disputing that, or whatever. It's just, sometimes I have to study, you know?"

"Wait, wait, wait." Ben closed his notebook and stared at her. "Your mom picked a fight with you this morning because you skipped a family dinner…to *study*?"

"Yes," Esther said patiently. "It's a whole thing."

"Like the Persian-not-Arab thing?" Ben joked.

He thought he might have overstepped, but, to his relief, she laughed. "Not quite as big as that one. No, they wanted me to get a business degree. They think my prospects would be better and my hours wouldn't be as bad—now or in the future." She shrugged, suddenly looking embarrassed. "Anyway. Sorry. Shall we?"

"No worries. Uh…where did you want to start?"

She closed her notebook and settled back in her chair. "Where do *you* think we should start? I'm not just going to let you coast off my work."

Ben sighed. Whatever he thought, they clearly hadn't been bonding. You…*really* don't think much of me, do you?"

"It's not…uh." She sighed. "It isn't that, so much."

"Could have fooled me." Ben raised his eyebrows.

"Okay, fine." She raised her eyebrows. "But, do you blame me? I don't think I've heard you speak up in class once. Do you know *anything* about the Quebec Bridge Disaster?"

"It was in 1907," Ben said promptly. "Everybody knows that."

"Everybody?"

"It was a drinking song during Frosh Week." Ben grinned at her wickedly. "Come on, don't tell me you weren't there… Or, wait, that sounds exactly like you. See? I can dish it out, too."

Esther did not look pleased by the joke—but, to his surprise, she didn't dispute it. She looked down at her notebook. "So, what were you thinking about the project? I thought maybe we could start with first-hand accounts." She smiled tightly and stood. "You research whatever you want, and we'll meet back here to make a plan for the project."

"Sure." Ben stood up. Her tone was frosty enough that Ben didn't want to spend any more time in close proximity. "You definitely aren't going to make the whole plan yourself and then complain that I'm not doing any work."

He stalked off through the stacks, but not before he caught sight of the hurt look that flashed across his face. Part of him was keyed up, ready for this, eager to score a hit—but another part of him felt sick to his stomach. What the hell was he *doing*?

He was showing her that she couldn't just walk all over him, his angry self told him. She couldn't just make accusations about his character and expect him to lie down and accept them. She'd been talking to him like she had him all figured out when she *didn't*.

And who was she to judge him, anyway?

He was supposed to be looking at books, and he stopped at random to look over the shelves. He didn't recognize any of the titles, of course, but he did know a fair amount about the Dewey Decimal system by now.

He sorted through topics in his head. Engineering tended to go under the 600s, in Technology, and bridges were... He scanned the numbers and titles under his fingertips, then checked a few stacks in either direction.

624, mostly.

He was beginning to get an idea, which was to look at the development of similar types of structures. He wasn't sure when the first cantilever bridge had been built, but—given the materials in question—it couldn't have been too long before the bridge disaster.

He flipped through a few books and discovered the Hassfurt Bridge had been completed in 1867, though it had been a much narrower design than the disastrous Quebec Bridge.

Maybe there hadn't been enough experimentation...

No. His research showed that another cantilever bridge had been completed over the Niagara gorge in 1883, meant for trains. That was neither an easy nor a low-stakes project, and the Forth Bridge had come along in 1890, using similar materials.

So, what the hell had gone wrong?

He was re-shelving the books with a frown when something caught his eye: something not bound in the same way. There was no title printed on the spine, and—in fact—the pages were handwritten. What was this doing in the stacks?

Ben opened it up and blinked. There were hand-drawn images of the bridge here. There were mentions of Quebec, little snatches of French...

"Esther?"

There was the sound of footsteps, and then she appeared around the edge of the stacks. "Yes?" she asked, in a much quieter tone.

"There's no one else here, you know," Ben pointed out. He snapped the journal shut and held it out to her. "This was mis-shelved, but I think it's an account from someone who actually worked on the bridge. Alec Durand. It's his personal journal."

"Wait, seriously?" Her eyes lit up and she came to look at it. "Not bad! This is actually pretty cool, and Durand—yeah, I know that name. He was overseeing things, he sent some telegrams and..." She scanned through. "I'll look this over."

"Hey, I found it." Ben raised an eyebrow. "Why should you get to read it first?"

She gave him a look.

"Okay, how about we split it?" Ben asked her. "The work, I mean. No one else is down here. I'll read aloud, you take notes?"

She hesitated for a moment, but nodded and handed it back to him. "I'll go get my laptop booted up."

"Cool." Ben strolled behind her, scanning the first page of neat, cramped script, with a header in a looser hand.

Alec, For when your words fail you, Love always, Ginette

Ginette gave me this journal on our wedding day. I don't know what to write, but she said if I put my thoughts down on paper, it might make me better at getting them out in person...

CHAPTER 6

The white boards on the outside of the church were freshly painted, and hydrangeas bloomed outside by the walk. Inside, parishioners and family packed the pews and stood in the back. It was a small church, already outgrown by its neighbourhood, and a wedding always brought in even more worshipers.

Alec stood at the front of the aisle and tried not to let his nerves get the better of him. He was not used to dressing this way, in finely-made clothes, and he knew that many of the people here were as much bemused by the match as anything. Ginette was a model of perfection, tiny and exquisite, quick with a laugh, her curly hair always escaping its crown of braids.

And Alec was…Alec. He looked down at his work-roughened hands and felt like a farm animal.

He was a labourer. He had always *been* a labourer—what else could a man be, after all, with such an ungainly body? He looked like a giant even when he was among other men, never mind when he was at Ginette's side. The people here must be staring at him, wondering what she saw in him, and when she came up to him and put her pretty little hand in his, they would shake their heads—

Don't think such things, Alec. He heard that admonition in her voice, always with the tinge of both humor and sadness. *They do not think such things about you, and you must not think them about yourself.*

They did, but he never argued with her. It was a miracle beyond imagining that she believed what she said. From the day they met, Ginette had spoken to Alec as if he had a quick mind instead of just strong arms. She had drawn out of him, without any effort at all, his dreams for the future. It seemed the most natural thing in the world to admit to her that he wanted to be an engineer, and when he heard the words out loud, cringing as he thought of her response, she had only smiled and told him he would make a fine one.

She had believed in him. She had been steady in her affections as he courted her. She had suggested a proposal—gently, but repeatedly. She had *not* wanted to wait until after he finished his schooling, either, but she had done so.

Alec had promised her a good life, and he would do anything in his power to give it to her.

The music started and everyone in the church who was not already on their feet, stood and turned, and Alec's heart gave a sudden sideways leap. He turned to look at the door and caught his breath, for there was Ginette, and she was more beautiful than he had ever seen her.

She and her mother had hidden away, working on this dress for months now. With delicate lace accents and beadwork, it was exquisite, fashioned with as much care as Ginette gave to everything. It was perfect.

She was perfect.

At the end of the aisle, she leaned forward for a kiss on the cheek from her father, who passed her arm to Alec with a smile. Unlike most, Ginette's parents did not seem to mind that she had fallen in love with a day labourer. Whatever made their middle daughter happy, made them happy, but they were still bemused.

Alec was simply glad they had not forbidden the marriage.

Then he stopped thinking of anything else, because Ginette was looking up at him with such adoration that he could think only of her.

The pastor made a gesture, and everyone who could sit, did so. The pews creaked and groaned. A few children spoke up and were shushed by their parents.

"Dearly beloved," the pastor began, and Alec's heart swelled. He held Ginette's hand and felt he might burst with happiness.

When it came time for the vows, he held his hand out for her to place the ring on his finger.

"I give you this ring," Ginette said clearly, "to wear as a symbol of our unbreakable bond. It is a reminder of my eternal faith and unwavering dedication. I will serve and protect you always."

Tears gathered in Alec's eyes and one spilled down his cheek. He could not help it, and he smiled when she reached up to wipe his face, standing on tiptoe. A few people giggled, and Ginette flashed them a smile, almost conspiratorial.

As if it had been a joke they were in on, instead of a joke *about* them. And, with just that, she seemed to transform it.

Truly, she was magical.

"I love you," she whispered to him.

"Alec," the pastor said, before Alec could respond, "please recite your vows."

Just like that, all his confidence disappeared.

Speaking. Speaking in front of a crowd. Alec had never trusted his words. They didn't come out quite the way he wanted them to, and worrying about it— when everyone was *already* inclined to see him as a big oaf—only made matters worse.

These were the most important words of his life, and he could hardly speak them aloud.

There was a little squeeze on his fingers, and he looked down to see Ginette watching him steadily. It wasn't an admonition, but a lifeline: *watch me, only me.* She held up her hand for him to slide the ring onto her finger.

"I…" Alec looked out at the crowd, and then back at Ginette. "I give you this ring, to wear as a symbol of our unbreakable bond." His voice was coming out more clearly now. "It is a reminder of my eternal faith and unwavering dedication." He stepped closer and had to work not to crush her tiny hands in his own. He could no longer hold in his smile. "I will serve and protect you always," he promised her.

Ginette's own eyes shone with tears, and she stood on tiptoe once more, leaning in for a kiss before the pastor had even told them.

The rest of the ceremony was a blur, with Alec's heart hammering nearly hard enough to drown out the sounds of cheers and clapping, and the triumphant organ music as he embraced Ginette.

"I love you," he whispered into her hair.

"And I love you." She looked up at him. "That was the most beautiful speech you've ever made."

"It was the most important." He looked into her brown eyes and wrapped his fingers around hers. "Also, I didn't have to come up with the words."

Her laugh was infectious, and a moment later, the two of them were swept away to the reception in the basement of the church.

Flowers had been picked from the gardens of the parishioners, and were set up in a mismatch of vases all over the room. Many of the women from the church had baked pies, while another had made a big bowl of punch. The parishioners cheered as Alec and Ginette fed each other the first bites of the cake, and then they sat on chairs decorated with ribbons and received well wishes from all their friends and family.

Cake gave way to dancing in little time, and Alec sat by himself at the head table as Ginette laughed and whirled with her family members. He did not dance—not ever, and *certainly* not now, next to the perfection that was Ginette. Though she beckoned to him, he shook his head and watched her, smiling. She was perfection, and there was no reason to sully it with his clumsy presence.

They were both beaming as they were swept into the carriage that would bring them home. They waved and gave a kiss as the carriage trundled off, to the sound of raucous cheers. Alec's face ached from how hard he was smiling.

His smile did not fade until they began to leave the picturesque neighbourhood behind. The elegant paintwork of the houses was no longer new, but faded and chipped. Then came houses that were smaller, older, not built with the same care.

Alec swallowed and held himself still. He had built a life for Ginette that he was proud of…until just this moment. He had cleaned the house from top to bottom before the wedding and everything was as wonderful as he could make it.

But the carriage continued, and the houses got smaller and in worse repair as they went.

Beside him, Ginette leaned her head on his shoulder and gave a happy sigh. "I wish this day could last forever."

"Truly?" Alec looked down at her.

"Of course." She looked up at him and wrinkled her nose. "Everyone we love there to celebrate with us, and we're going home to *our* home for the first time. I feel like my heart is going to…burst, I'm so happy."

Alec gave her a kiss, though he did not let it grow deeper. The carriage driver was pretending not to listen to them, but Alec still did not feel comfortable having the man see this.

Instead, he hugged Ginette close to his side and hoped that she would not be sad when she saw the house once more. She truly seemed happy, and he wanted to bask in that happiness—and see if he could find the trick to it, himself.

"I have a present for you when we get there," Ginette said.

"Oh?" Alec looked down.

"It's a surprise." She sat up to grin at him. "Though I'm not even sure you need it, after today. Well…I'll wait until you see it. I hope you'll like it."

"I'm sure I will," Alec promised her. He held out his left hand. "I very much liked the last present you gave me."

Ginette's peal of laughter brightened the air as the carriage came to a halt.

Here they were. It was a run-down house on a wide, unevenly paved street. The sky, which had been a gorgeous blue earlier in the day, was now grey and overcast. Thunder rumbled in the distance, and Ginette looked over her shoulder, holding her hat with one hand in the rising wind.

"Rain! Rain on your wedding day is meant to be a good omen."

Her spirit was irrepressible. Alec paid the coach driver and hopped down into the street before coming around to sweep Ginette into his arms. He went to the door and opened it one-handed, holding her easily, before carrying her over the threshold to the sound of her laughter.

CHAPTER 7

In the darkness of the main room, Ginette reached up to pull Alec's head down to hers. "I love you," she whispered.

Alec did not answer her in words. He let the kiss deepen, his arms curling to bring her closer to his body, and he shuddered with desire when she gave a little gasp of pleasure. Outside, the rain was just beginning, locking them into their own little world.

For a moment, Alec could see this room as it would one day be: bright and vibrant, with children running to greet him at the door and Ginette at the stovetop. It would be a proper home, filled with laughter and warmth.

The first drop of water down the back of his suit hardly registered, but when three more came in close succession, Alec broke the kiss and looked up at the roof, frowning. The mental image of the cozy house evaporated, replaced by cold reality: a run-down house on a run-down street, with drafty windows and a leaking roof.

He set Ginette down on the floor gently. "I'll go get something to catch that."

"Wait." Ginette caught his hands. "It's nothing. I don't want to think of anything but you today."

"I'll only be a moment." Alec kissed her and hurried to get a tin bowl from a cupboard. He came back and wiped up the drops of water with his handkerchief before setting the bowl in place. The next plink of water landed soon after, and he grimaced.

He should be able to do better than this for Ginette.

When he stood, she was holding a small gift out to him, wrapped in a piece of gauzy lace that he saw was her wedding veil. He unwrapped it gently, taking care not to let his callused fingertips snag on the delicate fabric, and found himself holding a leather-bound journal. When he opened it, it was to see a brief note in her elegant, sloping hand: *For when your words fail you.*

Tears pricked his eyes and he looked at her with a smile.

"I know you sometimes do not trust your words," she told him, and she came to touch his cheek. "And you think that you are lesser because you speak in deeds and not words. I have never had trouble knowing your heart or your thoughts, my love, but this is for you to practice your words."

"It's wonderful." It looked ridiculous in his giant, work-roughened hands, but that was not her fault. "I will practice."

"Now..." She was blushing as she plucked it from his fingers and set it on the table. "Enough about the roof and the journal. I told you, I want to think of nothing but you today."

His blood heated and he reached out a hand for her, but she twitched out of his grasp with a playful

smile and turned to run toward the bedroom. At the
door, she gave him a look over her shoulder, and she
was biting her lip—just the slightest bit uncertain.

He followed her with a smile and a silent prayer of
thanks to heaven that he had found this woman—and
that she, somehow, loved him just as much as he
loved her.

In the bedroom, she looked up at him uncertainly
while he closed the space between him. "I don't know
all of what to do," she admitted.

"I will show you." His words were sure with her;
they always were. He held her close to kiss her again
and felt for the buttons on her back. The sound of rain
striking the floor nearby made him pause, but he tried
to ignore it.

Their clothes came off with agonizing slowness,
until Alec thought he would lose his mind. A bared
shoulder, the soft skin of her wrist, the way her pulse
beat at her throat… This was like a dream. He knelt in
front of her and traced the path of her dress down
with little kisses while she shuddered and twined her
fingers in his hair.

But, as the rain increased, so, too, did the leaks,
until it seemed there was a tiny rainstorm in the
bedroom as well.

At last, Alec could no longer ignore it. "Give me a
moment."

"No." Her voice was halfway between stubborn
and plaintive, and she tightened her fingers around his
head when he stood, only breaking away when she
could no longer reach. Then, she took his hands and
drew him toward the bed. She was shivering in the

cold air and her skin was nearly luminous. "Stay here. Worry about that tomorrow, Alec."

He could not stop himself. He shook his head and hurried down the stairs to grab more bowls and pitchers, even a milk bottle. Half of his mind was already thinking about whether something was wrong with the posts that held up the roof, or if it was the boards, or the shingles—

When he looked up, it was to see Ginette watching him, blankets covering her nakedness, and he felt a stab of guilt.

"My love, I am so sorry—"

"I know the man I married." She sounded fond, if exasperated. "You could never leave something broken. I'm just lucky you aren't up on the roof in the middle of the storm, trying to fix it now." Her gaze sharpened. "Do *not* take that as an idea."

He laughed. "I promise. Perhaps I can make this brief pause up to you."

She gave him an impish smile. "Perhaps. I look forward to your attempt."

The next morning, Alec woke early. There were tiny shafts of sunlight shining through some of the gaps in the roof, though the containers on the floor were, thankfully, not full. The rain had passed quickly.

At his side, Ginette shifted sleepily and pressed herself against him; Alec kissed her shoulder with a sense of wonder. Part of him certainly wanted to stay in bed this morning…

But he would not be able to enjoy it, knowing that his new bride would wake up to a house with a leaking roof. If he got up now, he could begin some repairs while she slept. He eased his way out of bed and picked up fresh clothes from the wardrobe.

His eyes passed over the room as he got dressed. The floorboards could use another coat of polish, and the window frame should also be fixed. The wardrobe would almost certainly not fit all of Ginette's clothes, so he would have to make another. The only thing in the room that was still sturdy was the bed frame, and that was from necessity—Alec was too big not to take care with his bed.

In the kitchen, he set about making some coffee as quietly as he could. He added sugar directly to the boiling water and cut off a hunk of bread to eat with his coffee, then sat at the table to wait. He had missed leaks out here as well, though one seemed, conveniently, to be over the sink.

He pulled the journal over to himself as he chewed and flipped through the blank pages. They were creamy and soft, far more suited to Ginette's elegant words than his own, faltering ones, but he did not want to disappoint her. He went to get a pencil, one of the things he almost always had with him due to his role on construction sites, and tried to think of what to say.

Ginette gave me this journal on our wedding day, he wrote finally. *I don't know what to write, but she said if I put my thoughts down on paper, it might make me better at getting them out in person. She's probably right. Words don't come easily to me unless I'm speaking with her.*

He frowned for a second, considering, and tried to decide whether he should write as if he were speaking to her.

But *that* was something he could already do. Indeed, sometimes she joked that the only reason he had proposed to her was because they could have a real conversation, and that he would no doubt leave her for some rich heiress someday, once he was more comfortable with speaking in public.

The thought made him smile.

Words don't make very much sense to me, he continued. *I do not know how to pick the right word. There are too many meanings. When you build something, it is much easier. You can feel it under your hands. It bears weight and it stands or falls. Words cannot be measured.*

Words can hide lies, but materials cannot. When I can feel something under my hands, I can know that it is solid.

There was a drip behind him, and he sighed.

Solid…or not solid, as the case might be.

The coffee had brewed, and he drank down the scalding, too-strong liquid in silence before picking up his tool caddy and heading out into the early morning sunlight.

Once he had climbed onto the roof, the issues became clear: every piece of it had been shoddily built and would need to be fixed. Alec had been able to acquire some building materials from the off-cuts and leavings at the ends of various projects, and he set to work with a will. Small pieces of wood were shaped to fill cracks, holes in the tar paper were covered over, and new shingles were added to the patchwork on the roof.

By the time he caught sight of something out of the corner of his eye, he was coated in sweat, but very pleased with himself.

"Alec," Ginette said, sounding amused, "is this some honeymoon ritual I don't know about?" She stood in the street with a mug of coffee in her hand and a much more sensible dress than she had worn for the wedding. Her hair was caught back, but little curls escaped, and Alec took the time to smile at her before grabbing his tool caddy.

"I'm making sure there will be no more leaks," he said. He climbed down off the roof.

"Here." Ginette handed him a mug of coffee. "And there's fresh bread baking. One of the neighbours brought over some preserves as a wedding present."

"That was kind of them." Alec embraced her carefully, not wanting to get sweat on her dress, and kissed her forehead. "Wait. How long have you been up?"

"You really don't sense the passage of time when you're working, do you?" Ginette smiled. "It's mid-morning now, my love."

"My apologies. At least we have…" Alec looked up and sighed.

The roof would not leak again soon, that much was certain. It also, however, was made of so many materials that it had clearly been repaired many times. It didn't look so much like a patchwork quilt, he thought, as a mangy dog.

"I'm heading to the labour yard," he told Ginette.

"Today? But it's our honeymoon!" She looked up at him incredulously. "And you haven't even eaten anything—"

"Ginette, look at this place!" His frustration bubbled out of him and he waved a hand, somewhat desperately. "This is no life for you!" Mindful of the neighbours nearby, he drew closer to her and bent his head. "I promised I would do anything in my power to make you happy. I promised I would serve and protect you." He looked deep into her eyes. "We need a better place to live, and—"

"And we'll get there," she told him simply.

"But—"

"Come with me." She might be small, but the tone brooked no argument. She drew him into the small kitchen, now filled with the smell of fresh-baked bread, and flipped open a newspaper on the table. "There." She was pointing to an advertisement. "Like my father always says, work smart, not hard!"

He smiled and kissed her. "What would I do without you?"

She winked at him and pointed to the table for him to take a seat. "Now, get some food into you, before you head out!"

CHAPTER 8

Alec repeated the words of his pitch over and over to himself as he walked toward the job site. The rain had cleared and the day was warm, verging on hot. If he were working, he would roll his sleeves up and strip off his coat, but that was the sort of behavior for day labourers.

Which he, apparently, was not one of.

That was why he had studied as an engineer, after all, though he still liked to feel a building beneath his hands. Blueprints, he accepted as a necessary tool for buildings too large to conceptualize the whole of—or *touch* the whole of—at once. With each piece of a blueprint, however, he would let his eyes drift closed and try to imagine the materials under his hands.

There was a truth in buildings and structures, truth that was found nowhere else in this world. In Alec's opinion, creating a building and constructing it was the closest a man could come to God. Every tower, bridge, and even shack, was human ingenuity and strength, built from the world God had created.

Alec had never been able to put this thought into words as well as he was able to put it into the work of his hands, and he probably would have given up trying altogether, were it not for Ginette. Even when the engineering did not come as naturally to him as building, her faith kept him strong.

Her faith, and the simple facts of how the world worked. The man who built the buildings could only ever make so much, but the man who designed the buildings—he could provide well for his family.

Alec's lips moved again on the rehearsed line: Sir, my name is Alec Durand, and I am here to apply for the role of engineer.

He adjusted the briefcase a few times as he walked; his hand did not fit easily in the handle, and he did not want to hold it so tightly that he broke it. He was a man who looked at home hefting a sledgehammer or guiding machinery, but he could not shake just how ridiculous he looked when he pretended to be a businessman.

The city came within a few hundred yards of the construction site, but trailed away quickly to make way for the temporary structures that housed the machinery of the site. A few steel girders had been delivered, and one of the masonry pillars had been started, but the site was not yet filled with activity.

The activity would be provided by the veritable sea of labourers that clustered around a small platform, where a man with golden-brown hair stood smiling out at the crowd—the media photographers in particular. He wore his elegant suit with the sort of effortless confidence that came from a lifetime of easy living, Alec thought.

He told himself not to be hard on the man. Teddy Cardinal had designed a similar bridge some years ago, and it had been quite a coup for Quebec City to secure his services for this one. He most likely had a great deal to teach Alec.

"Mr. Cardinal!" one of the reporters called. There was a puff of smoke from flash powder, as photographers captured the event. "Did your work on the Hudson River bridge influence this cantilever design?"

"Of course!" Cardinal called back. He paused to flash a winning smile for the photographers. "As it should! It was an inspired piece of design, and quite a remarkable experience. Only God could have designed a better bridge!" He gave a jovial laugh and a wink, and dropped his voice slightly. "Or perhaps even God could not have designed one better!"

Alec shifted uncomfortably. He thought such jokes to be in poor taste, but he knew that many would simply say he was being superstitious. Cardinal came from a different world, much more sophisticated. He would naturally have different manners.

"What made you decide to hire the Phoenix Bridge Company for your construction crew?" called another journalist.

Contempt flashed across Cardinal's face so quickly that Alec was sure he had imagined it. Certainly, there was only a bland smile there the next minute.

"They were the best option presented," Cardinal said diplomatically. He paused to pose for another picture. "Our local consulting engineer, Mr. Archibald McDougall and I agreed on that." He nodded to the side of the platform, where McDougall no doubt stood; Alec could not see him through the crush.

More questions started, but Cardinal held up a hand.

"Thank you, gentlemen. That will be all for today—there's a great deal of work to do!"

He smiled and waved once more, pausing so that yet more pictures could be taken, and then he headed down the steps and pushed his way through the crowd, glad-handing the labourers and reporters as he went.

Alec watched as Cardinal made his way to a temporary office building overlooking the construction site. Nearby, steamboats were chugging past, and Alec could almost imagine them slipping under the bridge.

"Everybody!" The call came from the midst of the crowd, and the next moment, a man with dark hair and rolled up sleeves bounded up onto the stage. "Could I get your attention, please? I'm Archibald McDougall, and I'll be your site manager. We are now accepting general applications. Please line up here."

The men crowded and pushed to get to the front of the line.

"Form an orderly line, please!" McDougall called.

Alec stood firm as people tried to push him back, but the group did not so much form a line as a swarm, and there were dozens between him and McDougall.

On a sudden whim, he ducked out of the group entirely and made his way up the hill to the temporary structure. He was sure someone would call him back, but no one paid him the slightest attention. He was smiling as he approached the building and reached out to touch its walls.

The thing was crudely built, though it had been painted on the outside to make it seem well-constructed. Alec opened the door and closed it behind him with an excess of care, not wanting to shake the flimsy walls, and looked around himself. There was an open area with a desk, where a secretary might presumably sit, and a narrow corridor that led back to Cardinal's office. Alec could hear the man's jovial tones echoing down the corridor even now.

He imagined Ginette telling him to practice his words—and to stand up straight: *what, you think no one will notice you're tall if you slouch? Come now, my love, a tall stature is nothing to be ashamed of.*

He was trained, Alec told himself. He was trained, he was competent, and he could picture the elegant structure of the bridge in his mind's eye. He ached to make it real. He lifted his chin and headed down the corridor with a spring in his step, but frowned when he heard an angry tone. Alec could still picture the smile Cardinal had flashed at the reporters; what could have happened to make him so angry, in such short order?

Then Cardinal's words became clear:

"—More like the *only* option presented! When I think that these country bumpkins are now responsible for building the longest bridge in human history…" A sigh. "McDougall should have supported me with the Board."

Alec stared down at the floor. His ears felt hot. He had already considered himself a bumbling fool compared to the people of Quebec City—the clerks, the attorneys, everyone who wore crisp, white shirts and had soft hands.

He had wanted to become one of them—not for his own sake, but for Ginette's. If there had been a way to remain out in the sunshine and the fresh air while he designed buildings, Alec could have done that in a heartbeat.

But he wanted to give Ginette the life she deserved: one with a roof that didn't leak, a house with a fence and beautiful flowers, pretty china.

And here he was, listening to one of the very people he had looked up to…

Who thought less than nothing of Alec.

Alec unclenched his fingers—they had tightened, unconsciously, around the handle of the briefcase again—and then turned and walked out of the office. He closed the door behind himself with the same, exquisite care, and made his way down the hill to stand at the back of the line that was still progressing towards Archibald McDougall. There was a distant roaring in his ears.

"Hey." One of the men elbowed him in the side. "Why you dressed like that?"

Alec looked at him wordlessly.

"Some big shot, huh?" the man asked.

"Nah, saw him go up to the office…and then come back." Another man was laughing. "Did the big guy throw you out?" He looked Alec over contemptuously.

Alec said nothing. He simply took his jacket off and folded it over his arm before rolling up his sleeves. Then he stood in line and waited as the other men fell silent and the group dispersed.

By the time Alec arrived at the table, McDougall looked exceedingly bored.

"Name?" he asked.

"Alec Durand." Alec cleared his throat slightly, and then said, as politely as he could, "I'm very good with a sledgehammer, sir."

"I should guess you are." McDougall gave an approving nod at the breadth of Alec's shoulders. "Anything else?"

Alec did not let his gaze stray to the building on the hill. "No, sir."

○

"**O**kay, this seems pretty useless." Ben flipped the journal closed, though he kept his finger in to mark the place, and reached for his cellphone. "I bet I can find out more about this guy in 30 seconds than—ugh." He had forgotten there was no signal. What he *could* see, however, was the time. "It's 2:30! We've wasted three *hours* on this. Let's just go back to my apartment, we can use the internet from there."

Esther looked doubtful. "We haven't even learned what Alec did on the bridge yet."

"*Exactly*." Ben raised his eyebrows. "This is taking way too long. We're basically reading this guy's therapy notes. We know he wasn't the chief engineer, right? That was Cardinal. So…why spend hours reading about some poor schmuck with self-esteem issues?"

"Those who don't learn from history," Esther said precisely, "are doomed to repeat it."

Ben rolled his eyes. "Thanks, Churchill."

"George Santayana," Esther corrected him.

"Huh?"

"Santayana," she repeated. "A Spanish philosopher. He said it first and Churchill paraphrased him."

Ben was impressed in spite of himself. "No wonder you aced the last assignment."

He realized he'd made a mistake when she frowned, and he looked down before she could get a clear look at his expression.

"How did you know I aced it?" she asked.

"You're *always* at the top of the class, right?" Ben cleared his throat and opened the journal. "Anyway, you're right, let's keep reading. Where were we...? Okay."

CHAPTER 9

The jobs for the worksite were first come, first served—so the postings always said. But the next morning, when the cart pulled up, the foreman didn't bother checking to see which workers had come first. He scanned the crowd instead, while Alec watched nervously.

"You," the foreman called to a man with black hair and a surly expression.

Alec murmured a prayer under his breath. He had gone back the day before, intending to tell Ginette the truth of his new employment, but her hope had been too much for him to bear. He had said something about an apprenticeship.

If he went back without even the pay from day labour, he did not know how he could face her.

"You," the foreman said to a short, stocky man with sandy hair. His eyes came to rest on Alec and his eyebrows went up. "And you."

Relief coursed through Alec as he went to take his place on the cart, hauled up by the sandy-haired man; the surly one was sneering at both of them as if they—and the entire world—were nothing but an inconvenience.

He reminded Alec of Teddy Cardinal. The thought of Cardinal's derisive words made Alec close his eyes briefly, shame squirming hot in his chest, and he was surprised when the foreman jumped back up on the cart.

"That's all for today, men," the foreman called. "Come back tomorrow, all of you,"

There were a few angry mutters, but the cart pulled away too quickly for Alec to hear most of them. He leaned back against the side and was thankful that his stature at least qualified him for this work. He had no doubt that it was the main reason he was here—nothing more than an accident of birth, if truth be told.

The thought was demoralizing, but he told himself that he would work with anything he could get.

The cart came around a bend in the road, and there was the construction site. Alec narrowed his eyes slightly and tried to picture the bridge as it would be when it was finished; his fingers sketched the cantilevered design in the air. If he closed his eyes, he could almost feel the distribution of the weight along the trusses.

The foreman jumped down when they arrived, and the three new workers followed him down toward the site. With the faint breeze in the air, not to mention the coal smoke from furnaces and nearby boats, this reminded Alec of why he loved this sort of work. He enjoyed the smells of heating metal, and dust hanging in the air under a blue sky.

In any case, weather like this was far better than autumn rains or winter winds—for this site would keep working as long as possible, and Quebec City was not hospitable in the winter.

Alec looked up the hill to the structure that housed Cardinal's office, and allowed himself one moment of bitterness. He, Alec, would have been the sort of site manager the day labourers could respect: a man who knew both the theory within the engineering books and the reality of guiding a piece into position with pulleys and chains. He could have helped bring the bridge to life with both his hands and his mind.

But that wasn't going to happen, it seemed. He hurried to catch up with the foreman, and was directed over to where a group of men were using sledgehammers to pound a truss into place.

He worked steadily. The workers who were already part of the company weren't pleased to have a new person on their team, but Alec was strong and he worked hard, and so his companions' annoyance trailed off steadily as the morning progressed.

By the time the lunch break was signaled with a bell, his shirt was soaked through with sweat. As soon as he put down the sledgehammer, his arms burned and exhaustion dragged at him.

That was why Alec didn't stop working during his shifts: it was difficult to regain momentum once he had acknowledged the pain and exhaustion in his muscles. He wished he could have kept working, but his stomach was growling loudly, and the thought of rest and water sounded good.

He needed to prove himself to the foreman, after all, and hard work would only go so far if he then keeled over from exhaustion.

Lunch was taken in the shade of some trees by the riverbank, the whole group sitting on logs and crude benches. Some workers ate nothing but a hunk of bread, while others had pasties or, in one case, a spiced concoction with potatoes and peas that made Alec's eyes water. He was grateful, indeed, for Ginette's cooking: flaky pastry enclosing a filling of potatoes and beet, the sort of food he'd grown up on. It was something to keep a man full while he worked all day long, as his father used to say.

He had just finished eating when he saw a familiar figure, one in nicer clothes than the rest of the men were wearing.

McDougall.

Alec stood and closed his lunch pail, then wiped his hands on his slacks as he headed off toward the masonry pillar, on a path to intercept the site manager.

"Mr. McDougall," he called, once he was close.

McDougall turned to look at him in surprise, and there was some recognition there. "Ah, good—you were brought onto the team." He was nothing if not courteous. "Mister…"

"Durand," Alec said, and this time, he held out his hand to shake. "Sir, when I came yesterday, it was actually to apply for the role of engineer."

McDougall's eyebrows shot up. He looked Alec over.

"I can swing a hammer, sir," Alec said, a bit desperately. "I'm strong, and I'm a hard worker—"

"Mr. Durand." McDougall's smile was regretful. "While I have nothing but respect for what I'm sure are your very fitting qualifications—"

"Sir, I have my degree," Alec told him. He could feel his throat tightening with nerves. *Don't fail me,* he beseeched the words in his head. This was precisely the sort of time that they always fled from his mouth, leaving him gaping like a fish.

He swallowed and thought of Ginette, and the way her steady, warm gaze always loosened his tongue.

"I began in construction," he said, when he could speak again. "But I am well-trained, and I am acquainted with both the theory and execution of a cantilevered bridge. I could be very useful, sir. I would be an engineer who could work well with the men." He nodded to where the rest of the labourers sat, eating.

McDougall sighed. "Mr. Durand, the positions you speak of have all been filled—most of them yesterday, and the last one, this morning."

Alec swallowed hard.

Tell him how qualified you are, Ginette would say. *Tell him to make an exception, or take you on as an apprentice.*

But, staring at the man's clean, white shirt, all Alec could think was that this man clearly doubted him. Alec was a day labourer, not the sort of person who looked at home behind a desk, and McDougall was never going to see him as anything else.

He ducked his head. "Yes, sir. My apologies."

"None needed." McDougall smiled. "I'm glad to have someone of your skills working on this site, Mr. Durand."

He was gone a moment later, his mind clearly elsewhere already, and Alec stood, forgotten, watching as McDougall spoke with some of the

Kahnawake steelworkers—'Skywalkers', as most of the crew referred to them, based on the fearless way they navigated working at heights.

Cardinal, of course, was nowhere to be seen, now that the reporters were gone.

Alec returned to his work without a word. The crew was watchful—they had seen him speak to McDougall—but, again, Alec's silence and hard work won them over. By the end of the day, when he pulled out his fresh shirt and his suit jacket from a burlap packet, they had begun to address him by name.

And so, the days passed. Alec arrived at the selection site early, and rode on the cart with a rotating cast of other workers, as many as were needed for the day. He had been recommended by his crew leader, and so the foreman always picked him now, but Alec could only feel a deep stab of shame every time he pulled off his sweat-soaked shirt at the end of the day and went home to Ginette.

The time had long since passed when he would be able to admit to her what had truly happened, and what job he had.

It was three weeks later when he went home with his paycheck in his pocket and a deep exhaustion in his step. It shouldn't be this way, he thought, not with a new wife at home and a life beginning. He had always thought that an education was a pathway to steady work, but—as always—the connections between such things seemed to be built on a silver tongue and a secret sort of knowledge.

The sort of knowledge Alec never had.

Everyone in the church had been right to doubt him that day, while they watched him pledge his love to Ginette. He had thought so then, and he was only more convinced now. What she saw in him, he had never understood—

He opened the door and stopped, uncertain.

Ginette was standing by the table. She was biting her lip, resting one hand on the back of a chair. Normally, she would come to greet him at the door, tugging his head down for a kiss, but tonight she stayed where she was, with barely concealed joy.

"What is it?" Alec asked her. "Is all well?"

"I went to the doctor today," Ginette said. "Well, a friend of my mother's was there while I was visiting, and…" She smiled. "I have some news."

CHAPTER 10

There was a pause. Ginette's smile widened while she waited for Alec to understand what was happening, and Alec could not think of anything. The house looked the same as it always did. What could she mean? How could going to the doctor be good?

When she saw that he did not understand, Ginette gave a little laugh and put one hand over her belly. Her fingers splayed protectively, and she looked as if she could hardly breathe for joy.

Alec stood frozen, still in the doorway.

"I'm pregnant," Ginette said, misunderstanding his silence.

No. Oh, no. Alec held himself still so that he would not shake his head in horror. He was awash in self-hatred. This was his first child, a child with Ginette. He had dreamed of this day, and he knew it should be joyful. He had certainly always expected that it would be.

But today, when he had spent hours working with a sledgehammer, when he was bone-tired and had only meager pay to show for it, all he could think was that he was not ready for this. He was not the father this child needed, nor the husband Ginette thought she had married.

"Alec?" Ginette was beginning to realize that something was wrong.

"So soon," Alec managed. "I...never thought—"

Her face cleared and she nodded. "Yes. *Maman* told me that I should be patient, that it might take some months. I did not let myself hope when I began to feel ill." Her voice rose, exultant. "But it's true, the doctor confirmed it. We'll have a child, Alec."

Even his fear could not keep him from going to her then. Alec kissed her, bending down to hold her gently. He would have lifted her up, but for his fear that he might hurt the baby.

"I'm not made of glass, you know," Ginette murmured. She wrapped her arms around his neck. "You need not wrap me in wool for nine months."

"Perhaps I should," Alec teased her. He pointed to the corner of the kitchen. "I'll build you a day bed there, a throne, and you can order me about. I'll cook all of your meals and wait on you hand and foot."

"Mmm, that *does* sound nice." She sighed happily as he kissed her jaw and her neck. "Oh, Alec, you're happy, aren't you? Truly?"

"Of course, I'm happy. I dreamed of this life since the first day we met." Alec buried his face in her neck and inhaled the clean, sweet scent of her. "Is it a girl or a boy, do you think?"

"They say there's no way to tell," Ginette said, frustrated. "The doctors say so. They say that none of the old ways work. My mother swears that if I hold a string above my belly and see which way it sways—"

She broke off and looked up at him. "Alec. Truly. What is it?"

"Nothing," Alec protested.

When her delicate chin set mulishly, however, he knew he had lost the battle. Few people were more stubborn than Ginette—and surely there could not be any who were more stubborn than her pound for pound.

Alec stepped back and slumped into a chair. "The lead engineer for the bridge…"

"Teddy Cardinal?" Ginette perched on Alec's lap.

He nodded miserably. "He's some big shot from New York. He'd never hire a country boy like me."

Ginette frowned delicately. Then her expression settled, though it was not happy. She laid a hand on his chest and looked him in the eyes. "Did you not apply, Alec?"

Alec did not know what to say—and that was answer enough.

"Alec." She closed her eyes.

"I know, I know—I've disappointed you."

"You're a smart man, Alec!" She gave a little thump on his chest with her hand. "With a proper education as well. How are people supposed to *know* that if you do not tell them?"

"I did, I asked…McDougall. He's the site manager." Alec sighed. "All the positions were already filled."

"So, you *did* ask." Ginette leaned forward to kiss him.

"Yes. And it gained us nothing."

"No, it gained you *experience*." She cupped her hands around his face. "You know what I'm going to say, don't you?"

"That I should go back and ask again," Alec said, with a sigh.

"Yes." She kissed him deeply, and then reached down to press her hands around her abdomen. She was biting her lip, still smiling. "Oh, Alec... I am so happy."

Alec held her close and reached out to press one of his hands over hers. He could do this, he told himself. He had more reason now than he ever had to be brave, to go back and plead his case again. He could do it this time.

He *would* do it this time.

The walk back to the job site seemed to pass in an eyeblink. Alec could no longer feel his exhaustion, nor was there the usual whirl of anxious thoughts in his head. He felt almost the same way he did when he was working with the sledgehammer: eminently capable, as if his success was inevitable.

Teddy Cardinal might think little of the residents in Quebec City, but Alec would prove him wrong. He had studied the Hudson River Bridge extensively when the Quebec Bridge was announced. He knew a job site just as thoroughly as he knew the mathematics of it all, and he would do good work.

At any rate, he would not be at a disadvantage in Cardinal's eyes if all of his competition was from other locals.

One of the teams was still finishing up, and Mr. McDougall watched over them. He hadn't gone home with the rest, then; Alec liked that.

"Mr. McDougall?"

McDougall looked over and nodded. "Mr. Durand."

"Well remembered," Alec said, with a smile.

"Few people on this job site have quite such an impressive stature as you." A smile was playing around McDougall's mouth. "What can I do for you?"

Behind his back, one of Alec's hands clenched, as if he were bracing himself for pain. "I should like to be considered as a potential civil engineer, sir."

McDougall regarded him steadily, and Alec thought he saw genuine regret there. His doubts were back with a vengeance. "As I told you, there are no open positions."

"I know you did," Alec said. "But…"

"But?" McDougall raised an eyebrow.

Alec opened his briefcase and pulled out some documents to show them to McDougall. He caught sight of another worker watching them—Ralph, if Alec remembered correctly. The look on the other man's face was not exactly friendly.

"I recently completed engineering studies, and I've worked for several years in general labour," Alec said. "No professional experience in engineering yet, sir, but—"

"This is going to be the largest bridge in the world," McDougall told him. He looked up from the documents. "We cannot hire engineers with no experience."

"I understand that, sir." Alec swallowed. "But I am a hard worker. I believe your foreman will attest to that. And I will do whatever it takes to prove my worth. Please, sir—a chance is all I ask. I want to give my wife and child the life they deserve."

McDougall took a deep breath and considered, stroking his chin. "I can't in good conscience hire you as a civil engineer," he said finally.

Alec's heart plunged.

"*But*," McDougall said, "I could make an exception to hire an *apprentice*. It wouldn't pay much, but the experience would be valuable."

Alec wanted to laugh with relief. "Yes, sir. You won't be disappointed." He reached out a hand to shake.

McDougall, to his surprise, held his hand firmly. "See to it that I am not," he said, before shaking Alec's hand and gesturing for him to come up the hill. "Now, walk with me, we have some paperwork to fill out."

As Alec left, he was aware that Ralph was still watching them. The other man looked contemptuous and, out of the corner of his eye, Alec saw him shake his head as he went back to his work. Finally, he placed the man—the one who had jeered at Alec on the first day, mocking him for his suit.

Alec squared his shoulders. He would rise. He would make his mark on this project, and he would provide the life Ginette deserved.

CHAPTER 11

B en stopped reading and scanned the page. "Hey, can I see your notes for a second?" Esther hesitated briefly before turning her laptop.

Ben squinted at the notes. "Butterfly Effect?" Esther had typed that on its own line and highlighted it. "Like…the movie?"

"More like…" She screwed up her mouth. "In a real world, 'actions have consequences' kind of way."

"So…" Ben spun a pen in his free hand. "A butterfly flaps its wings in Peking and the Quebec Bridge collapses? I thought our opinion paper was supposed to be about ethics, not chaos theory."

"Whoa." Esther held her hands out. "Easy, there, Malcom."

"*Life, uh…finds a way.*" Ben held his hands out in front of him in his best Jeff Goldblum impression.

Esther grinned and proceeded to one-up him. "*So you two, dig up, dig up, dinosaurs?*"

Ben laughed. "I love that movie!" He'd never thought he would see Esther, of all people, do a spot-on Goldblum impression, but she was really pulling it off. He could feel himself relaxing and he leaned back to balance his chair on the back two legs.

"Me, too." From her smile, Esther was letting her guard down as well. "The first time I saw that T-Rex? I nearly peed myself."

"T. M. I." Ben pronounced each letter with emphasis.

"I can't believe I just said that." Esther sank her face into her hands, blushing furiously.

"It's okay." Ben let his chair down and leaned in conspiratorially. "I actually *did* pee myself."

Esther burst out laughing, startled, and Ben found himself staring. The carefree expression transformed her face. She seemed to have forgotten they were in the library, because he could not *imagine* her making noise like this if she remembered where they were. She was still chuckling as she tucked a loose strand of hair behind her ear—and then caught Ben watching her.

"Um." She looked uncertain for a moment, and then cleared her throat. "Anyway, all I meant was—with the butterfly effect, I mean—was that every word, every action, has a consequence. Even if you're the only one affected by something, the outward impact can be exponential."

It took Ben a moment to get his mind back to the topic at hand. He kept seeing Esther's easy smile and the happiness as she spoke about the movie she enjoyed. She was so careful to be focused only on school that he had never imagined her as *having* any other interests.

He cleared his throat as well. "Ah, right. Sure. But what does that have to do with the Iron Ring?"

Esther smiled and leaned across the table to tap the journal in his hands. "That's what we're trying to discover, Grant. Keep digging." She wiggled her eyebrows at him, then posed, hands over the laptop keyboard. "Fire away."

"We're mixing metaphors," Ben told her. "Anyway, you want to switch for a bit?"

"You don't approve of my note-taking?"

"No, I just thought maybe you could use a break." Ben shrugged. "You don't have to do all the work. We *are* partners, after all."

From the look she gave him, Esther thought this might be a trap of some sort. After a second, however, she nodded and handed the laptop over. When Ben gave her the journal, she opened it and scanned the page for a moment before beginning to read.

●

The day was beautiful. It was already hot, even with pools of shadow still gathering around every piece of equipment, but the breeze from the river and the clear blue sky kept things pleasant.

Alec watched the workers as he came down the hill. He had spent the past few days in the office, filling out various numbers into various forms—work that was not in the least bit challenging, but was very repetitive. He had no idea what his former coworkers had been told, and he had been nervous to face them.

McDougall had informed him this morning that several more numbers were needed from the labourers, and his expression told Alec that awkwardness would not be considered a good reason not to go acquire said numbers.

From a distance, the clamor and chaos of the job site faded away and provided the impression of a large machine. With each group making considerable noise, the entire job site held each other to a stable rhythm, meaning that sledgehammers and pulleys alike moved at predictable intervals, with the shouted commands of the foreman as a counterpoint.

Once he was in the clamor, however, Alec lowered his eyes. Was it his imagination, or were the workers giving him unfriendly looks as he passed? He turned to edge around a group and found a worker blocking his path. The man looked him up and down contemptuously.

"*Merde*. Are you lost, or are you looking for the circus?"

Alec said nothing and moved around him, but the laughter of the others followed him.

He spotted Ralph quickly and lifted a hand to him. "Ralph, a moment?"

Ralph looked him dead in the eyes and then turned away rudely.

"Ralph." Alec went to his side. "I need to know your daily counts for the rivet purchasing—"

Ralph looked over and took a drag on his cigarette before flicking the end of it at Alec's boots. He sneered.

Alec took a deep breath and looked down, trying to compose himself.

"Get a load of this one." Ralph was laughing. "He can't even look me in the eye! Tell me something, how does a dimwit like you get an engineering apprenticeship?"

The silence stretched until Alec muttered, " I graduated from—"

Ralph's guffaw cut him off. The other man had only been waiting for Alec to speak, precisely to talk over him. "We could replace you with an overweight mule and get better results."

Alec coloured and told himself to stand his ground. He needed to bring those numbers back to McDougall. He couldn't exactly go back and say the workers had made fun of him. On the other hand, the laughter of Ralph's team told him that no one else here was on Alec's side.

"If we wanted to work with an overweight mule," a new voice said calmly," we could just have hired your mother, Ralph."

Though the group had been ready to laugh at Alec, they were not shy about laughing at Ralph, as well. They roared with laughter and Ralph's face contorted before he stomped off.

Alec turned to look at the new man. He was taller than most, though not taller than Alec, and he had a tanned face with an easy smile, and long black hair braided down his back. He looked Alec up and down.

"Thank you," Alec said awkwardly.

The man nodded before putting out his hand. "Jean Beauvais."

"Alec Durand." Alec shook his hand.

"You must be that new apprentice everyone's chirping about." Jean had a lilt to his voice, something Alec could not easily place.

"I guess I am. Sir."

"Good manners." Jean flashed him a smile, teeth gleaming in the tanned face. "And don't worry about that goon. The crew can be hard on new guys—especially management. It comes from experience, and not the good kind. Come to me with those progress reports—I promise I won't bite."

"I appreciate it." Alec nodded at him. "My thanks."

"I'm not doing it for you." For the first time, he saw a warning in Jean's eyes. "I'm doing it for me...and the other workers. Someone has to keep an eye out."

Alec swallowed and nodded. He had thought for a moment that Jean might be an ally, a friendly face on the job site, but it seemed that chilly politeness was the best he could hope for. He watched as Jean walked away and then looked over to see a knot of workers watching him, Ralph in their midst.

What was there that Alec could do to...

He hurried after Jean, who had grabbed some of the riveting equipment.

"Here." Alec picked up one of the heavier pieces of equipment. "Let me help you." He hoisted the equipment onto his shoulder.

"Sure." Jean looked impressed. "Follow me."

The worker led Alec up a series of ramps and then stepped out, confidently, onto the bare girders that served as the highest level of support struts for the bridge. He did not so much as hesitate. Alec took a deep breath before following and tried to ignore the faint flex of the steel beneath his feet...only to catch a glimpse of the water below and stop dead. He grabbed support rods to steady himself.

"It's good to be scared of that."

Alec looked up. Jean was looking back at him.

"What?" Alec managed weakly.

"It's good to be scared of the drop," Jean said. "It reminds you what's at stake. Ncwatsíńen."

"En qua…sheen…nen?" Alec got most of the syllables correct, he was fairly sure, although he botched the delivery.

"Just some rules to live by on the job," Jean was smiling "Come." He beckoned Alec to a platform on the other side of the girder, where a furnace was throwing off heat.

The two men unloaded the equipment quickly and Jean laid it out.

"First rule up here," he said, looking up briefly, "is to pay attention. Understand the site and proper procedure. It's all there because someone else learned the hard way. Last thing you want is to be that guy."

Alec managed a chuckle and a nod.

"Second rule," Jean said briskly, "is to keep the site tidy. Your mother isn't here to pick up after you, and a hammer in the wrong place could mean the difference between here…" He gestured to the platform. "…And there." A wave of his hand took in the water.

Alec looked, and immediately wished he had not done so. The water, which seemed to rush predictably along when he was on the ground, now seemed as if it were surging up toward him, rising with each pulse in his ears—his own heartbeat, hammering so hard it was drowning out everything else.

"Hey, big guy." Jean tapped him on the shoulder. "You all right?"

"…Good. I'm…good." Alec managed to refocus on Jean's face.

"Good. How's that furnace coming?"

"Uh…" Alec stoked the flames. He watched the colours shift and the meter climb, and then nodded to Jean, who helped him dump a bag of rivets inside.

"Third rule," Jean said. "This one is the most important, so pay attention: don't be stupid."

Alec recoiled.

Jean smiled and held up his forearm, where a dark red scar traced over the muscles. "Sounds easy, right? And that's why it's easy to take for granted. But I got lucky with this burn. We can't afford any mistakes up here."

Alec nodded. He looked out over the water, and then back to Jean. "Ncwatsíńen." This time, he pronounced it more exactly.

Jean gave him a quick handshake and Alec made his way back without looking down at the water. The rest of the riveting team was climbing up, and Alec thought that they greeted him more respectfully than the workers had earlier.

It was progress, at least. Alec headed back toward the office building with a lighter heart and a sense of purpose. He could do this, he told himself. He would prove himself to McDougall—and to the entire crew.

CHAPTER 12

Without realizing it, Ben had stopped typing. He was staring off into the middle distance, and he only came back to reality when Esther leaned over into his field of view and waved a hand.

"Uh. Sorry." He shook himself.

"Is it something you'd like to share with the class?" she asked, amused.

"It's not—well, it's just something that happened when I was a kid." Ben forced a smile.

He had thought Esther would let it go, but instead, she closed the journal and leaned on her elbows on the table.

Ben considered. "It's not even a big deal. I left some Legos out in the living room and my dad stepped on one. He yelled at me about it...then my mom yelled at *him*. He stormed out." Ben sighed. "He didn't come back for three days."

"Three...*days*?" Esther looked lost.

It was always an unpleasant jolt to speak to someone who didn't understand these sorts of things. Ben could tell from Esther's expression that her father had probably never stormed out for days at a time. Had she ever even overheard her parents fight? Probably not.

And, while she only looked startled now, it would turn into pity or judgment soon enough. It always seemed to. People started to think they knew things about him because of what his family life had been like when he was little. It had started with the teachers, who seemed like they had gone out of their way to remind Ben of the divorce and the fights every time he managed to forget. They had *said* they wanted to cut him some slack so that he could get through a difficult time...

But, instead, what they had done was see problems everywhere. They told his mother he was struggling with the transition, when the fact of the matter was, they had just started watching him like a hawk and assuming they knew everything about him.

He had seen the process play out dozens of times over the years, and he *especially* didn't want to see it happen with Esther...though he wasn't sure why he should feel worse about her doing it, than someone else.

He could think about that later. He distracted her by flashing a smile. "Too bad I didn't have those job site rules back then, huh?"

Esther considered this. She folded her arms and took a deep breath. "You can't control other people's decisions, though," she said finally. "Your father made *his* choices, but you can make your own."

"That's some sage wisdom." Ben managed a smile. "You should write a book."

"Maybe I will." She gave him an impish grin.

"I'll be first in line for a signed copy," Ben told her.

"...Really?" She looked a bit confused.

"Oh, yeah." Ben's smile widened. "The signed ones go for more online."

She crumpled up a piece of paper and threw it at his head while Ben laughed. He had distracted her successfully, but he found that he also liked her laugh. He watched as she picked up the journal again and opened it up, and he was smiling as he got ready to take more notes.

"Where was I?" Esther muttered. "I noticed you were spacing out...here. So, I'll go back a few sentences. Okay."

○

Alec spent enough energy focusing on his path down the walkways that he was on solid ground before he noticed McDougall watching him. The site manager was holding a roll of blueprints and looked manifestly unimpressed with Alec.

Alec looked down at his clothing, expecting to see grease stains or dust, and looked back up curiously when he realized he did not look any the worse for wear. He was sweating, but then, anyone would be after a climb up onto the bridge, wouldn't they? And he had stayed with Jean, so it wasn't as if he had been doing something unsafe.

"What were you doing up there?" McDougall asked him.

"Oh. I was just helping Jean—one of the workers." Alec pointed up to where Jean's team was now pounding rivets into place. The group had a well-established pattern, tossing rivets through the air, catching them in leather buckets, and pounding them into place on the girders. He was still watching them when McDougall said,

"That's not your job, Mr. Durand."

Alec swallowed and looked down.

"Do you have your reports done?" McDougall asked him. He held up the hand with the roll of papers. "I need to sign off on the updated blueprints from Mr. Cardinal."

"No, sir." Alec flushed with shame. "I'm sorry, I—" He looked around, as if he might come up with something to say if he just looked elsewhere; then Alec caught sight of Ralph watching him. The other man had a smirk on his face, as if he were entirely unsurprised to see Alec having difficulty with McDougall.

Alec broke off and looked down.

McDougall cleared his throat. "Mr. Durand."

Alec looked up and saw a warning in the other man's eyes—as well as a surprising amount of understanding. The understanding, somehow, only made him feel worse, however.

"Sir, I—"

"This is not a popularity contest, Mr. Durand." McDougall spoke quietly, though his voice was firm. "Everyone on this site must perform his own role to the strictest standards. We have a responsibility here, not only to this corporation, but to every citizen of this country, and our neighbours to the south, who will be shipping goods across that bridge."

"Yes, sir." Alec looked down at his feet. He could not bring himself to look McDougall in the eyes.

"Come," McDougall said. There was no rancor there. "Show me what you've got so far."

Alec trailed behind him as McDougall strode up the hill to the offices. McDougall walked as if he had no doubts that this was where he should be—an engineer, a valuable piece of the organization that would assemble the bridge.

Alec, meanwhile, wondered if he had any place here at all. He had thrown away his place in the piece of the process he knew, and he was already failing in his new role. Jean had not saved Alec from Ralph— no, Ralph was the only one who had seen the truth.

The self-indulgent train of thoughts was broken only when he nearly walked directly into the closing door. Alec caught himself and went to his desk. He was very aware of McDougall's eyes on him. The report was on his desk, partially completed, and he felt a wave of annoyance at the sight of his own writing.

No. He must finish the form.

"A moment, please, sir." He tried to keep his voice level as he filled in the numbers Jean had just given him.

Instead, McDougall came to look at the form over Alec's shoulder. He traced his finger down the lines of the report and then gestured for Alec to stand aside while he took the chair, unrolling the new blueprints and checking numbers against one another.

Alec stood nearby, fidgeting and trying to tell himself that McDougall's frown wasn't getting any deeper.

When McDougall looked up, however, Alec knew that he had just been lying to himself.

"Where did you get these numbers?" The site manager looked like he was ready to read Alec the riot act.

"From the men, sir."

McDougall stared at him for a moment and then looked back at the report. He was shaking his head as he pulled the comptometer over to him and began punching in numbers.

"The numbers aren't correct," he said, as he scribbled down calculations on a piece of scrap paper.

"I...I'm sorry." Alec swallowed and watched McDougall. The other man was continuing to work with an ease that said he had done each of these calculations many times. He didn't have to stop to double-check his equations, like Alec did. He could just make the leap from numbers and paper to a full building.

Alec had the trick of that with his hands and raw materials, but it still wasn't easy for him to picture things from a blueprint.

McDougall snapped his fingers at Alec without looking up, and Alec snapped back to attention.

"Yes, sir?"

"What is the yield strength for steel?"

"Uh, I...I have it somewhere." Alec began shifting through the pieces of paper on the desk.

"As an apprentice, you should know these material yields like the back of your hand." Now there was a touch of annoyance in McDougall's voice. "These are essential components of the bridge and must be accurate."

"I'm sorry, sir." Alec came up with the correct book and ran his finger down the page. "312, sir."

McDougall came to look at the book. As Alec had, he traced his finger down the page. When he saw the number, he was still for a moment.

"This can't be right," he said finally.

"Sir?"

"This suggests the rivets will exceed maximum tensile strength." McDougall took a deep breath "Did you know that?"

"I..."

McDougall seemed to be regaining his equilibrium. "Mr. Durand, do you understand how vital this is? If even one of these numbers is a fraction of a percentage off, there could be a disaster."

"Yes, sir." Out of his depth, Alec tried to think what he could say. "I was...very precise with these numbers." He had been. He had checked and double checked them.

"Indeed." McDougall did not sound like he believed it. "But it is very difficult to remain focused when you're hanging about, yes?"

Alec swallowed.

"I will complete the report." McDougall did not smile. "That will be all, Mr. Durand."

Alec hesitated, then left with a nod. Outside, he listened to the clamor from the work site.

He sighed and ran a hand through his hair. His first week, and he was already making unforgivable errors. He would go back later, he decided, and see how the form had been completed. Then he could learn from his mistakes.

Hopefully, he could also repair Archibald McDougall's poor impression of him.

"**B**enjamin O'Betany to the front desk, please." The voice echoed over the intercoms. "Benjamin O'Betany."

Ben looked up from his reading with a frown.

"Was that for you?" Esther asked him.

"Nah." He had no desire to find out what was going on.

"Benjamin O'Betany to the front desk, immediately. Benjamin O'Betany."

"It's definitely you," Esther said. "Go on."

Ben groaned and stood up. "Okay. I'll be right back."

He took the stairs two at a time up to the main floor and jogged over to the desk, where he stopped dead with a blink. "Tyler?"

CHAPTER 13

"What's up, loser?" Tyler grinned at him. "Came to give you something."

"What?" Ben frowned at him.

"This." Tyler leapt at him and tried to get him into a head lock.

Ben laughed and ducked out of the way, then caught a glare from one of the librarians, who was presently checking the intercom system. That moment of distraction was enough for Tyler to get an arm around Ben's neck. He started rubbing his knuckles in Ben's hair.

"Yeah, you left this at home," Tyler continued. "Thought I'd—" He broke off with a yelp when Ben managed to get a pinch in on his ribs.

"*Shhh*," the librarian said, annoyed. There were multiple staff members at the intercom desk now.

Tyler rolled his eyes at her, not even bothering to hide his disdain, then grinned back at Ben. "No, but seriously—saw you balls-deep in that book with your *study buddy*." He added jazz hands for emphasis. "Figured I'd help you bust out of jail."

"You got the front desk shook," Ben observed. "Was that you on the intercom?"

Tyler looked immensely self-satisfied. "Yep."

"*How?*"

"This way." Tyler jerked his head down the little hallway that led to the atrium and stopped at a landline on the wall. He picked up the receiver. "I saw them punch in the code once. Wanna try one?"

"Nah, I'm good." Ben was grinning, though. Tyler was a font of tricks just like this, which had made their childhood together much more fun than it would have been otherwise. Ben stretched and sighed. "Thanks for dragging me out of that basement, though. Felt like I was turning into a mole or something."

"No problem." Tyler leaned against the wall. "Ti-Cats are playing tonight. I could probably get tickets off some locals pretty cheap?"

"Yesss. I've been studying all day. Do people really do this all semester? It's exhausting." Ben shook his head. "Let me just go finish up with Esther."

"Oh, so it's *Esther* now?" Tyler arched one eyebrow.

"Yeah, she's not as bad as I thought." Ben shrugged. "In some ways, totally a bummer, but—yeah. Does a sick Goldblum impression."

"Nice." Tyler, a fan of anything campy, wasn't going to argue with Esther's taste on this count. "All right, I'll see ya back at the pad."

He and Ben did their old secret handshake, ending with a fist-bump explosion, and Ben headed back into the basement. He really was getting tired, he thought as he walked down the stairs. Tyler had still been asleep when Ben left the room this morning, and Ben wished he'd had the opportunity to sleep in, as well.

Sleep in, and then play some Mario Kart instead of studying. What were Saturdays for, after all?

Esther watched him come back through the stacks, polite concern on her face. "Is everything okay?"

"Oh—yeah, it was nothing." Ben pulled out the chair and sat. "I, uh…had some books on reserve that came in."

"Oh," Esther's eyes flickered to where Ben was, notably, not holding any books, but she didn't mention the fact.

There was an awkward pause, and then both of them spoke at once.

"Well, uh—" Ben scratched at his shoulder.

"Is it okay if—" Esther broke off. "Sorry."

"Nah, go ahead." Ben gestured to her.

"Sorry, it's just that I have to get ready for work." She looked at her watch. "Do you mind if we pick this up tomorrow?"

Thank God. Ben didn't want his relief to show on his face, so he tried to cover for it with mock-disappointment. "Aw, man. I was having such a good time. We were making progress!"

"Yeah, you…weren't a total idiot." Esther gave a slow, considering nod. "I'm pretty surprised."

Ben threw his pen at her and she laughed, ducking out of the way with a speed that told him she either had a friend like Tyler, or siblings.

"All right." Ben held out his hand for the journal. "I'll go sign it out."

Esther gave him a look.

"What?"

She flipped the book around to show him the metallic stamp on the inside of the back cover. "It's reference material, we can't check it out. They don't let these go."

Ben leaned forward to get the book and frowned at the stamp. "Yeah," he said, after a moment, "not a problem."

"…What?"

"This is simple magnetic coding." Ben laid the book out flat and put his phone over the magnet before opening his laptop. "Easy enough to get around."

"What are you—" Esther lowered her voice and leaned forward. "What are you *doing*?"

"I hacked into the induction coil software a few months ago." Ben shot her a grin. A few lines of code appeared on the command prompt and he copied them out before making a careful correction and hitting enter.

"Gotcha," he muttered, as the screen flashed a single word. He swiveled the computer to show Esther the message reading COMPLETE. "Problem solved."

"Ben. Ben. You can't do that."

"Do what?" Ben stood up and started packing his bag.

"You need to undo that." Esther was packing her bag, as well, but she kept looking over at the journal. "Ben…"

"It's fine," Ben told her, amused. Ready before she was, he dropped the journal into his backpack with an exaggerated expression, then zipped the backpack up and headed for the stairs.

"Ben!" Esther hissed.

But he was already at the stairs. He chuckled to himself as he climbed. Did Esther *really* not do anything like this? Ever? Of all the things in the world, she *must* have kept books checked out for too long, right?

No, she was probably the type who read all her books during the original check-out period, and got citations for her term papers, so she wouldn't need to check the books out again. Ben groaned and looked heavenward. Just being near Esther was exhausting.

"*Ben.*" She caught up with him as he got to the top of the stairs.

"Yes?" Ben asked innocently.

"You can't do this!" Esther looked vaguely panicked.

"Wow." He looked her up and down. "You're really worried, aren't you?"

She shot him a paranoid glare.

"Esther, it's just a book."

"That doesn't—that isn't why I'm—that doesn't make it *better*."

"And it's going to work *just fine*." Ben turned around and shimmied backward through the security gate, keeping his eyes locked with Esther's. Her mouth dropped, and he was fully through before she realized the alarm wasn't going to go off.

Ben gave her a mock-salute and headed out into the spring air, only for her to catch up with him.

She didn't say anything this time, just looked at him with a worried expression.

"Here." Ben swung the backpack off his shoulder and took out the journal, handing it to her. "Would you feel better if you held onto it?"

She sighed before reaching out to take it.

"You haven't signed a deal with the devil, you know," Ben told her, amused. "You're just making sure we have a book available for studying tomorrow. ...Tomorrow. A Sunday."

"Do you need to be at church or something?"

"I need to be *asleep*," Ben said plaintively. He waved his hands. "But I'll be here. Suffering."

"Good." Esther did not look up from where she was scanning through the journal.

"Really, your concern is getting embarrassing."

She shot him a smile at that. "Right. So, tomorrow?"

"Same time. And don't read any without me!" Ben jabbed a finger at her and was surprised to realize that he actually meant it. He didn't want to be left out of the discovery. It was easy to say, from this side of history, that something had been wrong with the bridge—but how long would it take Alec to figure that out?

"I won't read ahead." Esther held up one hand.

"Fair enough." Ben waved and headed off toward the apartment, already chanting one of the Ti-Cats cheers under his breath.

CHAPTER 14

"Come on, man." Ben grimaced. "Don't—no, don't—oh."

Tyler gave him a cheeky grin and took the clipboard the saleswoman was offering. He filled out the credit card application with his usual insouciance, but nothing was going to make it a quick process.

Ben looked over at the stadium. The sun was setting now, and the sky was pale, but the floodlights would be on soon. He should probably have worn something warmer under his sweatshirt, but beer would help...or, at least, make him care less about the chill in the air.

"Eh? Eh?" Tyler reappeared, doing a slow turn. He pointed at his head, where a yellow-and-white beanie was now perched.

"You got something on your head." Ben gestured.

"I know! Free hat, just for filling out that stupid application." Tyler tried a couple of dance moves.

"I am so embarrassed for you right now."

"Oh, come on. Seriously, what d'you think?"

"I think you get what you pay for," Ben said, with feeling. He ducked, laughing, when Tyler took a swipe at him. "You look ridiculous."

"Eh, you're just jealous." Tyler adjusted the hat. "Come on, let's do this! I wanna grab a beer before kick-off."

Esther sat on her hands and tapped her foot while the printer ran at a snail's pace. She had spent the past hour and a half filling out forms, and no amount of efficiency on her part fixed the fact that the form was poorly designed, and the database was a nightmare.

She had written up several pages of potential improvements, all of which had been shelved as there were no resources available to improve the systems and redesign the forms. At a non-profit, that was understandable—but still frustrating. They, of all people, needed to be able to operate efficiently. Esther had investigated how she might make the changes herself, but with the workload at school, this project kept slipping.

And now the school year was almost over and so was the job. By this time next year—hell, within a few weeks, probably—she would be at an engineering firm and some other student would be doing the work that Esther had done.

Frankly, it was work that almost anyone could do. She had taken this job because she believed in the mission of the organization. With homes being built for underprivileged families, it had seemed like just the thing for an engineering student. She had been disappointed to find out that she had no opportunity to offer suggestions on structural design, materials, or anything else that would use her fledgling talents, but she had stayed out of a sense of obligation.

In retrospect, she would probably have made more money working in a coffee shop.

Her parents didn't even approve of her having a job, really. They pointed out that she didn't need one to pay any bills, and that her scholarships were based on academic performance, which could only suffer based on extracurricular activities.

Even her rebellions were boring. Esther sighed and rubbed at her face. Was Ben right about her? Did she leap to conclusions and, meanwhile, do nothing of note? She had been focused entirely on school when she should have been focused on—

Actually, she wasn't entirely sure what else there was to focus on. She had been to a couple of parties over the course of university—well, she had walked past them—and they really didn't look like much fun. Very loud. Bad beer. Smelly.

The document was finished printing. Esther reached out to take it and slipped it into the relevant file. She put the file in the stack to give to her boss, and then swiveled in her chair and started on the next form.

○

The crowd was roaring, and Ben jumped up and down with them, pumping his fist in the air to the rhythm of the chant. His throat and his feet both ached, but he didn't care. He and Tyler leaned toward one another, yelling in unison:

"Oskee wee, oskee wa wa! Holy mackinaw! Tigers! Eat 'em raw!"

On the edge of the field, the Ticats' mascot Pigskin Pete led cheerleaders in the team's time-honoured chant. Gold, black, and white pompoms waved, as cheerleaders tossed their hair in unison before forming up for the finale. With kicks, stomps, and a shimmy, they ended their halftime routine to the cheers and whistles of rowdy fans.

Ben looked over at the scoreboard as the two teams jogged back out onto the field. "Tight game."

Tyler didn't pay attention for a moment; he, like many other people in the stands, was booing the Montreal Alouettes. When he did turn back, he flashed a smile Ben's way. "Eh, they're losing, and they know it."

"That guy doesn't know it." Ben jerked his head toward a man in the row behind them. One of the few in the stadium dressed in a red, white, and blue jersey, he also had a huge flag that he was waving…and a very loud, off-key voice. His ability to stay on pitch was hindered by the fact that he seemed to be several beers in and was trying to avoid getting drowned out by the far more numerous Ticats fans.

Tyler snorted. "Yeah, I'm surprised he's still alive." He tossed a contemptuous glance over his shoulder. "Does he know what stadium he's in? In fact…" He wiggled his eyebrows at Ben.

"Oh, boy." Ben couldn't resist a chuckle. "Here we go." He turned to watch as Tyler swiveled around and gave an overly cheerful wave at the Alouette fan.

"*Bonjour*!" Tyler exclaimed.

The man's glance took in Tyler's Ticats hat, and he waved the flag boldly in Tyler's face. "You like the flag?"

Tyler tapped at his ear. "*Je ne comprends pas*," he said innocently.

The Alouette fan gave a derisive snort and waved the flag in Tyler's face again. "There you go, little boy—hey!"

With a cheeky grin, Tyler had yanked the flag away, and he waved it in the man's face.

When the man lunged at Tyler, Ben restrained him. "Hey, now."

The man didn't so much as spare Ben a glance, lunging again for Tyler, who threw the flag onto the field.

"What're you gonna do??" Tyler taunted the Alouette fan.

The fan didn't give it a second thought. He wound up for a punch and put his whole weight against it. Tyler ducked easily, but Ben hadn't seen the punch coming. Heat and pain exploded across his right eye and he fell, spots in his vision.

He had the sense of the crowd pulling the man away, and there was a swarm of security team members, some of whom marched the drunken fan out of the stands. Between the jeers of Hamilton fans and the game resuming, everyone had forgotten Ben completely. When he stood up, clutching his eye, it was to see Tyler laughing and shouting insults at the Alouette fan.

Tyler turned back and gave a guffaw at Ben's face. "Loser," he taunted.

"Dude, what the fuck?" Ben stared at his friend for a moment before shaking his head and sitting down in his seat.

"You okay?" Tyler asked, his attention still half on the field. "That was—whoa, whoa—YEAH!" He pumped his fist for the Ticats, who had just scored, and the rest of the stands leapt to their feet.

The only one still sitting, Ben leaned his elbows on his knees and frowned.

●

The house was quiet when she got home. Esther slipped her shoes off and put them on the rack, then headed to the kitchen for a snack. She could hear the distant sound of Yasmin chattering away to her friends.

There were granola bars in the cupboard, so Esther grabbed one of those and an apple from the counter before heading upstairs with her backpack still slung over her shoulders. There was still light under her parents' bedroom door, and she paused to listen. She could hear them doing a crossword puzzle, a habit they had both picked up to learn English and had kept doing together since then.

Esther hesitated before knocking lightly on the door.

"Come in." Her mother sounded curious. When Esther popped her head around the edge of the door, both of her parents looked surprised. They were sitting in bed together, both in their pajamas, the book of crossword puzzles open between them.

"I just wanted to say hello," Esther said awkwardly. "And good night."

Her father smiled at her. "Good night, dear."

"Did you get a proper dinner?" her mother asked immediately. "I left a plate for you in the fridge."

Esther held the apple and granola bar out of view. "I ate, don't worry."

"Esther Emami, I have known you since before you were born, I know when you're lying."

Esther grinned shamefacedly. "I have an apple. I'll bring the leftovers for lunch tomorrow. Thank you for packing them. I'm sorry I missed dinner, I just don't want to leave the office without help until I have to. They haven't found anyone to replace me."

Her mother's face softened slightly. "I know, my dear. Are you able to go to bed now?"

"I should study."

Her father put a hand on her mother's arm to stop her from making a retort. "Remember to get enough rest," he told Esther diplomatically. "My father always said, after 10PM…"

"Go to bed, sleep will help more than studying," Esther finished. The advice had served her well. "I'll make sure to get some sleep. Goodnight."

In her room, she slumped down in her desk chair and wolfed down the granola bar and apple. She was hungrier than she had realized, but she didn't really want to go back downstairs and heat up an entire plate of food, so she pulled out her journal and wandered over to her bed.

Once there, she opened it and stared at the blank page before flopping back on the bed and staring up at the ceiling—and the Jurassic Park poster. She could do a re-watch while she did some homework, she supposed, but the idea didn't really appeal. Neither did writing in her journal.

In fact, she couldn't think of anything she really wanted to do right now other than read Alec's journal, and she wasn't going to do that without Ben.

She looked over at her backpack and chewed on her lip. Maybe...

No. She had promised him.

And she was definitely too stir-crazy to sleep. Esther rolled her head sideways on the pillow and stared at the various things on her bookshelves: old textbooks, a pack of cards, a tiny statue of an elephant, a mug with a picture of the London Eye.

Everything was changing, she told herself. It made sense that she was feeling strange and unsettled. It would all feel better soon.

She just wished she could be sure of that.

CHAPTER 15

"Ben? …Ben?"

Ben startled and sat up. He had gotten to bed late the night before and had proceeded to lie awake for what felt like hours. Now he was leaning back against the wall in the basement.

"Hi, sorry."

"What's with the sunglasses?" Esther asked, as she sat. As per usual, *she* looked well-rested and professional.

"Nothing. Uh…" Ben took one of the two coffee cups in front of him on the table and slid it toward her. "I thought maybe you'd like one of these."

"Thanks. That's really nice. I don't really drink coffee, though. I'm so sorry."

"No worries. More for me." Ben pulled it back and downed as much of it as he could in one gulp. His glasses slid out of place as he did so, and he took them off when he put the cup down. He rubbed at his face before he remembered the bruise and winced.

"What happened to your face?" Esther sat up, looking worried.

"Nothing." Ben waved a hand. "I…football game, accident. You know how it is." He cleared his throat. "Did you end up reading any further in the journal?"

"Nope." Esther's answer was so quick that he could tell she had thought about it. She held it up and smiled at him. "It didn't feel right to read ahead without you there."

"It wouldn't have been," Ben said, mock seriously. He couldn't say why, but his mood had just lifted considerably. He pulled out his laptop and opened it. "I'll pull up the notes document. You want to get started?"

A lec pushed his way in the door and smiled when Ginette leapt at once to her feet. She was heavily pregnant by now, and had been telling him how much her joints ached by the end of the day. If she was moving so well, she must be feeling better—

"Alec," she said, her face drawn.

His stomach dropped. "Are you well? Is it the baby?" He was crossing the floor as he spoke, laying a hand on her belly and the other on her cheek. The house was a mess, he thought distractedly. His tools were lying about, and Ginette didn't have the strength to do all of the housework right now. They should get a maid.

"It isn't—" She stepped away, one of the only times she had ever done something like that. "I heard something today. I can't—"

"My love, what is it?" He reached out to her. "Come, sit. Have you eaten?"

She shook her pale face and bit her lip. She did not move when he gestured to the chair, and finally she turned and began to pace around the room. "Alec, it's about—the bridge."

Alec relaxed slightly. With her manner so distracted and worried, he had feared that this would be something to do with her parents, or his, perhaps another squabble with one of the neighbours. He knew that Ginette was lonely here sometimes, and that she wished he worked shorter hours, but she had always understood when he told her that this was the time for him to put in longer hours to prove himself.

Ginette twisted the fabric of her skirt between her hands as she paced anxiously. "I was in town, that's where I heard it. I was on my way back home after seeing the doctor. I wanted to stop by that café you like to get you something special for dessert tonight…"

She stopped pacing and her eyes grew far away as she recounted the event. In his mind's eye, Alec could see the bustle of people in the café. He could almost smell the tea and the fresh pastries and see how the afternoon light would slant across the floor. The pastries there were too dear for them to afford, but Ginette knew how he loved them; he felt a pang of guilt in his belly.

"I overheard two men talking," Ginette said. She wouldn't face him. "They were at a table with all these papers, and they were arguing. At first, I didn't listen—out of politeness—but then I heard them mention the bridge. One of them was blond, his clothes were very expensive, and the other had brown hair—"

"McDougall," Alec said softly. "And Cardinal. Cardinal was the blond one."

Ginette nodded jerkily. She bit her lip. "Yes. The dark-haired one—McDougall—he said that there was some issue with the length of the bridge, the...span?"

Alec nodded.

"And Cardinal told him that the bridge had been extended in length because the company couldn't afford to build...piers where they needed to be." Ginette's voice dropped on the words, and she came over to sit now. "He wasn't worried, he was trying to get Mr. McDougall to stop talking, but he didn't, he said he was concerned by the stresses from the length."

Alec swallowed and tried to slow his heartbeat. He told himself that all was well, and that Ginette was simply worried by words she had not understood—but now McDougall's worry from the other day was coming back to him in clearer focus.

"Mr. Cardinal was very angry," Ginette said. She was twisting her apron in her hands again. "He said it was wrong for Mr. McDougall to criticize him in a public place, and then he started..." She was scowling now. "He was so derisive of us, Alec, you should have heard him. He spoke as if no one here was his match. But that's not the important part. He said that McDougall's criticism put him in the place of a subordinate, and he could not accept that. He said...he said McDougall should clear out his desk and resign his position. And then he stormed out."

Alec sat frozen.

"I confronted him," Ginette said fiercely.

"You did what?" Alec's voice rose in panic. "Ginette—"

"I had to!" Ginette flared up, her chin set. "I asked him why he would not even look at the numbers the other man had put forward. I said Mr. McDougall wouldn't have made those numbers up for no reason. But he told me to *control* myself, and that you and the crew were safer than on any other work site!" She clenched her hands. "Alec, you have to...to do something!"

"To do what?" Alec asked her quietly.

"Ask him! Find out what's happening. The dark-haired man, he said the bridge could *collapse*, Alec!" She had started to cry. The skin around her nose and behind her eyebrows had flushed bright red.

"It's not going to collapse." Alec reached out to hold her gently by the shoulders. "Look at me, Ginette. I'm safe. The bridge is *not* going to collapse. Mr. Cardinal has far too much experience to allow something like that."

But she wasn't reassured. She only shook her head, stray curls flying. "Then why would *he* say it, Alec? And why would Mr. Cardinal fire him?"

"I don't *know*!" Alec reared back and sank his head into his hands. "I have no idea, Ginette. I wasn't there."

"So go ask—"

"D'you really want me to risk my job?" He looked up at her now. "Right now, when we're starting to raise a family? He fired McDougall on the spot. That could happen to me."

He had hoped for her to nod, to look understanding. When she only shook her head, however, his temper began to rise.

"Alec, *please*." There were more tears in her eyes. "Please speak to him."

He closed his eyes against the rush of anger. "I need...some air."

She cried out as he stood up to leave, but he didn't look back. He made his way to the door as if he were drowning, and the only air in the world was outside.

The sound of a clank and a scream made him whirl around, however, and he gave a cry at what he saw: Ginette, lying prone and still with blood trickling down her forehead. She had tripped on one of the hammers that was lying out, and had caught her head on the edge of his toolbox, and now—

"Ginette?" His voice quavered and he dropped to his knees beside her. "Ginette! Wake up, please— wake up!"

CHAPTER 16

Esther stopped reading and looked up, stricken. "Oh, wow."

"What do you mean, 'oh, wow'?" Ben demanded. "Don't say that! Keep reading!"

"Right." She looked down at the page, and she was smiling a little bit.

"What are you grinning about?" Ben asked her suspiciously.

"Nothing. Just you, getting all invested, Mr. 'It's a Gimme Course.'"

"Yeah, yeah, whatever—just keep reading."

The hospital waiting room was an abomination of faded, dirty pinks and greens. Cheap curtains were patterned with poorly printed flowers and the lights were flickering. It was late now, and even the summer daylight was fading.

Alec leaned back in his chair and passed his hand over his upper lip, where sweat kept beading. With his hat on the chair beside him and his coat unbuttoned and dirty, he felt even more out of place than if he had simply been here in his labourer's clothes. This place seemed to magnify every piece of him that didn't belong.

His hand was aching. He loosened it and remembered the clipboard in his grip. Several forms were crumpled at the edges and the blank fields stared at him like a reproach. He had left Ginette, pale and still, with the doctors, and he could not even finish these forms?

That galvanized him. Despite his hatred for the sloppy look of his handwriting, he began working. The pen kept slipping in his fingers, ink blotches staining them.

Alec, please, please—

Ginette! Speak to me! Wake up, please, my love. Please.

His mouth trembled and he continued working. He spent all day filling in forms, but these were unfamiliar to him.

Why would he lie?

Her name, her date of birth, whether she had any usual illnesses…

—worried about the stresses—

He gritted his teeth and tried to keep writing, but there was a winking light at the corner of his vision: his wedding ring, lightly scratched, with a gleam that made him furious and guilty all at once.

Please—

The pen slipped out of his fingers and went clattering to the floor, too loud in the evening stillness. Alec scrabbled after it, clipboard clutched awkwardly in one hand, and stopped only when he saw the pen fetch up against a pair of polished, black shoes.

The owner of the shoes was a doctor with salt-and-pepper hair, somehow immaculate despite the hour. He looked briefly at his own clipboard.

"Mr. Durand?"

"Yes! Yes." Alec stood hastily.

The doctor's eyebrows raised when he took in Alec's full height, but he made no mention of it. "Mr. Durand, I have just come from your wife's bedside."

"Is she—"

"Resting. The baby is fine." The doctor smiled reassuringly. "We'll monitor her to make sure everything heals properly, but there should be nothing to worry about once she's discharged."

Alec's shoulders slumped. "Thank you, doctor."

Unexpectedly, the doctor stooped to pick up the pen. He handed it back to Alec with a small smile.

"Right now, what she needs is rest. We've given her something to ease any pain and help her sleep." He inclined his head. "This way."

The room, now that the nurses had left with their lamps, was even dimmer than the waiting room had been. A single electric light flickered on the wall. In the bed, Ginette lay still. She looked as small as a child, almost impossibly frail, and only the rise of her pregnant belly hinted otherwise. White gauze had been wrapped around her head, and, while it should surely look ridiculous, Alec thought it looked rather like a crown—or a halo.

Alec reached out a hand to touch her cheek, and then drew back, mindful of the doctor's admonishment. Ginette needed rest, not more of Alec's clumsiness. If he had not left out those tools, she would still be well.

There was a rickety chair next to the bed and he sat down with a sigh. He should likely go home, but he could not bring himself to leave. If she were to wake and be alone—

No. No, the true reason was that spending the night here, uncomfortable and sleepless, seemed like the beginning of a true penance for his actions. Alec fixed his eyes on the cross above the door and began to pray.

It was agonizing, the way the night passed. The sounds outside the building and in the hallways slowed to almost nothing. There were times when Alec heard raised voices—and, once, the pound of feet—but there did not seem to be other visitors here this late.

He completed the forms and set them on the rolling cart next to the bed, and then he paced the room with trembling hands and sweat seeping through his shirt and his suit jacket. Ginette hardly stirred, but every movement was like a balm to his soul.

When at last she stirred, her eyes fixed on Alec immediately. Her lips moved, but no sound came out.

"Water," Alec said. He hurried to pour a glass from the pitcher at her bedside and helped her sit up to sip at it. He wanted to fold her up in his arms, but he forced himself only to support her. When she finished drinking and leaned against him, he breathed in the scent of her hair and tried to calm his racing heart.

"Alec, what happened?"

"I left out my tools." His voice was thick. "They got in your way and…oh, Ginette, I am so sorry."

She looked up at him, worried and pale. "I don't remember much—"

"The doctor said you need rest," Alec said firmly. "And I will see about getting you some food. Just lie back, my love. You and the baby are both well, don't worry."

"The baby." She pressed her hands against her belly and smiled, though there were tears in her eyes. "They said so? They said the baby was fine?"

"They did," Alec assured her. "I will go fetch a nurse and be back in just a moment, my love."

Out in the hallway, he leaned against the wall and shook.

Ginette wanted him to be safe. He could not help but shudder at the memory of her panicked face. She wanted to make sure that he was well. What with her feeling so ill, perhaps she was taking this experience harder than she would, otherwise. And, hadn't her mother told her, more than once, that it was easy to get caught up in tears during a pregnancy?

Yes. He must make sure not to worry her any further. She was in a delicate condition. It was his own fault that she had worried so much already. He should have soothed her, promised her that all would be well, said whatever he must to placate her. She need not know the frustrations of working for a man like Cardinal.

When he returned, he would do everything in his power to help her see that he was safe. He would not get frustrated or repeat the mistakes that had led to her injury.

Ginette and the baby were the two most important things in the world, after all, and far more important than Alec. He would not do anything that might beggar them, and he would not let them worry about him.

He would make this right.

CHAPTER 17

"Hey, let me see what you've written." Esther reached out for Ben to push the laptop closer to her.

"…Why?"

"I'm just checking your notes." Esther looked like this was the most natural request in the world.

To Ben, however, it rankled. "They're fine, back off."

"*Ben*." She rolled her eyes. "I am trying to make sure we're capturing both your thoughts *and* my thoughts so that we can refer to them later."

"Oh." Ben wasn't sure if he was mollified or embarrassed. He cleared his throat and sighed. "I should—wait a sec."

Esther's project was still on his desktop. If she minimized the screen, even by accident, she would see it. Ben held up a finger and tapped at the keys as quickly as he could.

"I…got an…email." Once it had been safely stowed in a folder, he spun the laptop around. "There you go."

"Uh…huh." Esther gave him a skeptical look before scanning over the notes. She mouthed words to herself as she went, a habit Ben wasn't sure she was aware of. He thought briefly about bringing it up, but didn't want her to stop doing it. It was surprisingly adorable.

"Maybe we should add something about him leaving the tools out," Esther said, when she finished. She held her hands poised over the keyboard. "May I?"

"Sure, sure. But why?"

"If he had put them away…" Esther was typing, frowning at the screen. "…Then she wouldn't have fallen."

"Hey, now—yesterday, when I told you about the Legos, you said it was out of my control."

"No." Esther stopped typing and looked up at him. "I said you couldn't control how your parents reacted. Leaving the Legos out was your fault."

Ben shrugged, surprisingly nettled. "Maybe people should watch where they step."

"Okay." Esther held up one finger and then started typing. "Okay, here. The Code of Ethics. The first point reads as follows: Hold paramount the safety, health, and welfare of the public…" She swiveled the laptop back around to show him the webpage.

Ben leaned forward to read for a moment, then gave her a look. "…Within the workplace," he finished.

Esther sighed and ran a hand through her hair. "Okay, yes, but—we're going for a larger point, right? Alec was an engineer, and this engineering project…" She moved her fingers in a circle, telling him to complete the thought.

Instead, he returned to an earlier point. "Okay, but let's say a guy forgets to lock his door one night, and his house gets broken into, and he's robbed and killed. Are you saying he's responsible for his own death?"

"No!" Esther threw up her hands. "No, there's a difference between negligence and...ignorance. Leaving your Legos out when you're a kid? Ignorance. You didn't know that could hurt someone. Forgetting to lock your door? Ignorance. A mess-up. Leaving your tools out, though, when that's something you're specifically trained to do, *and* it causes a safety hazard...that's negligence."

"Okay, but I read an article the other day that— hang on a sec." Ben pulled out his phone and began typing a search. "Dammit, no signal."

"Uh-huh." Esther looked amused.

"Let's go outside." Ben tapped on the table and shut his laptop with a decisive click. "Come on. We have the journal; we don't have to be in this hellhole."

"You just want to be somewhere with an internet connection, and I'd like to point out, that's not exactly conducive to us finishing in good time."

"Come on. Sunshine! It'll be great." Ben gestured for her to stand up and slid his books into his backpack. When she sighed and began to pack up her things as well, he smiled to himself. Esther really wasn't used to anyone pushing back when she said things.

Would she just have *given* him the Materials assignment if he had asked?

The thought made him uncomfortable in ways he could not put a name to. He shook his head and swung his backpack over his shoulders, then trudged up the stairs in silence beside Esther.

They emerged to a pink sunset. Ben tilted his head and found himself relaxing into the view—until his phone started vibrating in his pocket non-stop, causing him to jump and flail.

Esther looked over at him in alarm.

"One sec." Ben fumbled for his phone and began trying to unlock it. Messages kept coming through, all of them from Tyler, and he read them aloud one by one.

Got a date for tonight!
Check the fridge, think we need booze
If there's no Corona, get some
She's bringing her friend by the way
Hello?
Dude, don't tell me you forgot about the party

He grimaced when he was done, and Esther smiled.

"I'm guessing he...didn't tell you about the party?"

"Yeah, he likes to keep my life interesting." Ben shrugged as he slipped the phone back into his pocket. "Hey, you wanna come?"

"Me?"

"You see anyone else here?"

Esther looked confused and worried, as though this might be a trap. She looked away. "I can't. Not tonight."

Ben waited, one eyebrow raised.

When the silence grew too much for her, Esther shook her head. "I really can't. I have to do tomorrow's readings, there's a test next week I need to study for… Not to mention, there's all the notes we took today, and I need to organize those—you'll have to send them to me, by the way—"

"Whoa, whoa, whoa." Ben held out both hands. When Esther stopped talking, he edged forward and put his hands on her shoulders, much as if he were calming a fractious horse. "When was the last time you took a night off?"

From the look Esther gave him, he might as well have been speaking Greek. "Um," she said succinctly.

"I know we're here to go to classes and do homework and all that, but being a student doesn't have to be your *whole* identity," Ben told her.

"But we *are* students."

"Until we graduate, which is in like two weeks. Then it's all: 'get a good job, have kids, pay your taxes.'" Ben did finger quotes to emphasize the instructions. "What are you going to do then? Will you not go to parties then, either?"

"I…don't understand the question."

"Esther, we're human beings. We work to live, not live to work. You don't wanna look back on the best years of your life and be filled with regret, right? You don't want to remember that you spent the whole time with your nose buried in some book."

"What, it's better to get wasted and be a rebel?" Esther tilted her head.

"Yeah, yeah. I know you think I'm just a slacker, but trust me, one night off isn't going to ruin your GPA. Anyone's GPA, really, but *especially* yours."

Esther had narrowed her eyes.

"It would be fun to hang out with you," Ben admitted finally. "Maybe we could watch Jurassic Park…?"

"Right." But Esther was smiling now. "Okay, fine."

They stared at each other awkwardly for a moment.

"Does it start now?" Esther asked.

"Not for a bit. But I need to go grab beer. You could come with me?" Ben raised an eyebrow.

"…Sure." She looped her thumbs through her backpack straps.

"You really haven't gone to any parties, your whole time here?" Ben knew he sounded incredulous. He was incredulous.

"There was never time," Esther said defensively. "Engineering is a hard major. And it's a competitive field once you graduate, they do look at your transcripts. I mean…I guess I figured I could do that stuff later. If I wanted to."

"You never wanted to?" If Ben's eyebrows went any higher, they'd climb right off his forehead.

"Not really. Bad beer? Loud?" Esther shook her head. "And, I mean—some of the people in the Redsuits are okay, but aren't their parties the worst ones?"

"Best," Ben corrected her. "The *best* ones. Their parties are *legendary*."

"Okay, I'll bite. What, exactly, is legendary about them?"

"I don't know, it's…" Ben waved his hands. "There's the beer."

"Of course."

"And some of them are in a band," Ben pointed out, "so there's music."

"Good music?" Esther looked skeptical.

"Uh. They're alright. Singer graduated last year, though. But, the parties are an institution, so *everyone* is there." He looked over. "What are you thinking? You're frowning more than anyone I've ever seen."

"I'm wondering what…happens at parties. What does everyone talk about?" Abruptly, she looked self-conscious.

"You don't have to guess, you know. You'll see one tonight."

From her expression, Esther was about half a second away from fleeing.

"Hey." Ben stopped her and turned her gently to face him. "And if you don't like it, that's what the Jurassic Park offer is for, right?"

The tension went out of her, and she nodded.

"Okay. Now, let's go get some beer." Ben grabbed her hand and pulled her along towards Main Street, whistling as he went.

CHAPTER 18

The nearest LCBO did enough business from the university students that it was a wonder anything was still in stock…or that the students had any money left from their financial assistance. Ben guided the cart along the aisles. With the requested Corona now in their cart, he could look for something else, something Esther might like more.

"So, what do you like to drink?"

Esther bit her lip. "I don't know. I like wine sometimes. I'm not much of a drinker, to be honest."

"Ahh, so perhaps something a bit smoother…?" Ben raised an eyebrow and reached out to grab a bottle of Schnapps. "Ever seen Cocktail with Tom Cruise?" He flipped the bottle up into the air.

Esther clapped a hand over her mouth, and then gave a relieved giggle when Ben caught the bottle without a single fumble. When he pulled another bottle off the shelf with a meaningful look, she made a hand gesture to stop him, but his second flip, this time with two bottles, was just as successful, leaving her shaking her head and looking over her shoulder for any staff.

Ben laughed and grabbed a few things to put in the cart. "My dad and I used to watch it all the time," he explained. "He actually showed me how to mix drinks like that in high school."

Surprise flitted across Esther's face, but she tamped it down immediately. "Your dad sounds like an interesting guy." Curiosity filtered through.

At least it was curiosity, and not pity, but Ben didn't really want to engage with either. This had been about getting to know her, not giving her a window into a broken family. Instead of answering, he pointed over at the rack of cider. "How about that? You like cider?"

"I don't...really know." She shook her head helplessly. "Sorry."

"Well, tonight you try some. If you don't like that...tequila." Ben gestured at the bottle in the cart. "But we'll try the cider first. Wine is for moms and vampires."

"That's...an interesting combination." She tilted her head to the side, and then grinned at him. "So, if you got transformed into a vampire, you'd have to start drinking wine? Or...wait. Am I a vampire?"

"Can't be," Ben said, after a moment of thought. "I've seen you too many times in direct sunlight."

"That would make me a mom, and I'm *pretty* sure I would have noticed that."

"Okay, fine. Wine is for moms, vampires, and the terminally lame." Ben grinned as Esther hit him on the arm. "Come on, let's get this stuff back to the apartment."

The walk back was thankfully quick, but both of them had aching arms by the time they got all of the booze up to the apartment room. Esther set her bag down with a relieved sigh and rolled her shoulders.

As she looked around the room, though, she pressed her lips together.

Ben saw the common room in a new light all of a sudden. Plastic cups and old pizza boxes were piled near the coffee table, and there were empty chip bags, half-eaten breakfast sandwiches, and class materials spread all around the room.

He winced and began picking up. "Sorry for the mess. Seriously. I...didn't realize it was this bad."

"The fish is not aware of water," Esther said calmly.

"More of your sage wisdom, huh?" Ben stuffed the things he was holding into an overflowing garbage can, and pointed. "Why don't you go into my room. I'm going to throw this out and I'll be there in a sec. It's...*less* of a disaster." He found himself hoping that his recollection was correct.

When he returned, it was to see Esther standing on his bed—a bed that had been, suspiciously, made up. Ben was very sure he hadn't done that.

Whatever the case, Esther was looking over an interconnected collage of photos, clearly entranced, and a quick scan of the room showed that she hadn't picked up anything else. Her shoes sat neatly by the door.

"What's this?" Esther asked him, looking over her shoulder.

"Well, it *started* way back in elementary school." Ben began picking up dirty laundry and throwing it into the hamper. He tried to focus on the pictures instead of the state of his room; it was better than the common area, but not by much. "Tyler and I put it together for some project, and then I just…kept going with it, I guess."

He hopped up on the bed to watch with her and leaned in, purposefully close enough that he could brush against her. She jumped, but didn't say anything, and he saw her cheeks flush.

He wanted to be smooth about this, but he found himself too flustered to say anything suave. Instead, he cleared his throat—was he blushing, too?—and said, "Yeah, the project was…third grade, maybe? Tyler and I have known each other since first grade, though. Our parents got divorced around the same time. Whenever one of us needed to get out of the house, we'd just meet up and raise hell."

Esther's face lit up. "Oh? Like what?"

"I mean, we were seven," Ben pointed out. "So, the usual for that age: ring someone's doorbell and run away, stuff like that."

"Ah." She looked almost disappointed. "I thought maybe you'd be some skateboard punk spray painting graffiti everywhere."

"Oh?" Ben leaned against the wall, his hand pointedly covering up one of the photos.

Esther's eyes narrowed and she pulled his hand away, laughing, to reveal a newspaper clipping of Ben and Tyler's high school prank: "GRAD 2016" spray painted on the roof in 20-foot letters.

"Aha!" Esther announced triumphantly. She leaned forward to look, and her eyes traced down to a picture of Ben and Tyler on their first day of high school, standing together in front of the school. "You look so sweet and innocent in this photo!" she told Ben. "Tyler, on the other hand, looks like…"

"A little shit?" Ben suggested.

"Your words, not mine." She held up her hands, laughing.

"Yeah, well, he was." Ben gave a fond smile. "He's always had my back, though, you know? Everyone needs a friend like that. The person you'd call to bail you out of jail...but you couldn't, because they'd be in there with you, talking about how awesome it was." He was grinning when he looked over at Esther, and his smile dropped abruptly when he saw how she reacted to it. The people he hung out with had always thought that saying was the epitome of friendship, but something about Esther was making him reconsider a lot of things right now.

"Uh...*huh*." Esther looked over at some of the other photos. "So, tell me about these. They've gotta be old, especially this one." She was pointing at a very old black and white photo of a couple cutting their wedding cake.

"Oh, yeah. I swiped those one weekend while I was visiting my dad." Ben's smile had faded. "They were back in this room full of old stuff, family heirlooms and all, and he never went in there, so I knew he wouldn't miss them. I always liked old photographs, always wanted to see people's photo albums. The people in really old photographs always look so serious and it makes me wonder what they're thinking, you know?"

He could hear himself talking, but his mind was faraway. The project had sent him and Tyler rummaging through their family photo albums. It was one of the first times Ben could remember that he hadn't even tried to talk his father into agreeing to something.

He'd just snuck into the storage room and looked over the photos, taking some home at random—whichever caught his interest. Later, he scanned some of them and got proper copies printed, but he had returned the copies, not the originals. The albums hadn't been touched for years before he got there, and there was no indication that his father even noticed them missing.

Other photos had made their way in over the years. There was a cluster of pictures of Ben and Tyler. There were beach photos, pictures of them on their respective first bikes, and class photos with some people scribbled out. There were some members of Ben's mother's family, well-known members of Quebec City's social scene in the 20th century; trips Ben had taken, one of him sleeping with sharpie on his face, and dozens of others, a series of moments he couldn't classify easily.

"Are you close with your family?" Esther asked quietly. "You said you loved looking at photo albums, your grandparents must have liked that."

"My mother's parents, yeah." Ben came back to reality. "My dad's parents both died when I was pretty young, but they were always…distant…before that. Long line of engineers, actually." He managed a smile.

"Your dad, too?" Esther sounded intrigued.

"Yeah. I asked him to give me my Iron Ring for the ceremony. Who knows if he'll actually…well, anyway." Ben shrugged. "What about you? Any engineers in the fam?"

"Nope." Esther looked glum. "I'll just ask Professor McLeary, I guess. My parents were pretty surprised when I chose it as my major, but...I guess you could say I'm a bit of a rebel." She looked oddly proud of herself for that.

Ben, who could only think that Esther was one of the most well-behaved people he'd ever met, found himself biting his tongue. Her parents had gotten annoyed at her for doing too much homework, apparently, so maybe she really was driving them up the wall with her straight A's. He couldn't imagine it at all, though.

And, when he didn't respond, Esther hunched her shoulders awkwardly. "So, when's the party supposed to start?"

"Well, Tyler won't be home for another hour or so." Ben hopped down from the bed. "Should we read another entry, check in on our main man Alec?"

"I'd like that." Esther took his hand to get down and pulled out the journal. "Do you want to take notes or read? I kinda like it when you read."

"Oh?" Ben held her gaze.

She flushed. "I mean, then I can take proper notes."

"Uh-huh." Ben opened his laptop and balanced it on one arm as he put in the password, then handed it to her. When she settled down on the bed, laptop on her legs, he made sure to sit close to her to read.

He was smiling as he opened the journal.

CHAPTER 19

Alec frowned as he punched numbers into the comptometer. He wrote the result down carefully on the form and frowned. It was done. He wished he could be surer of his numbers. Once, he would have brought the form to McDougall, or to one of the other junior engineers—but with McDougall gone, there were few people who even tolerated Alec's presence, let alone helped him.

Not to mention, sometimes he thought there were whispers that it was his numbers that had gotten McDougall fired. Perhaps it was only his imagination, but…

A sound caught his ear, and he looked toward Teddy Cardinal's office. Alec had thought the other man was alone, but he could hear him talking.

Shaking his head, he went back to his reading. Some of the struts did not seem to be behaving as expected, and it was difficult for Alec to focus on. Ginette was recovering well, but she was so heavily pregnant that she could hardly sleep these days, tossing and turning. Alec didn't think he'd had a good night of sleep in weeks, and though he was sympathetic, he also spent most of his days wanting to curl up under his desk and rest.

He heard the noise again and gave up on reading through the rest of the report. He would hand the reports to Cardinal, who would probably be angry, but it occurred to Alec that perhaps he could simply hand the reports over and leave, especially if Cardinal was in a meeting.

That idea was appealing. With the looming medical bills, Alec worried about his job every day. He did not want Cardinal to be angry about his numbers the same way he had been angry about McDougall's. He could not afford that. The one time he had tried, speaking up after a meeting, Cardinal had given him a once-over and had warned, without any subtlety at all, *I wouldn't emulate McDougall too closely, you know.*

Alec stood up and made his way quickly down the hallway, coming around the door to see—

Just Cardinal. Alec cursed internally before realizing that Cardinal hadn't noticed him at all.

"We need the bridge to span the river, Mr. Cardinal," The American said in a mocking falsetto. His eyes were a bit wild, and he looked as if he'd slept in his clothing. His voice switched back to its regular register. "Very well, I have a design for that, a flawless design. *'But we can't afford that, Mr. Cardinal, isn't there any way to reduce costs?'* Try this design instead, gentlemen. I think you'll find it satisfactory. *'But, but...'"*

As Alec stood transfixed, watching the pretended conversation with a mixture of fascination and worry, Cardinal grabbed at his head and gave a groan of frustration. As he tore at his hair and pulled, a clump came off in his hand and he stared at it, horrified.

Alec was frozen. He wanted to leave. He didn't want Cardinal to see him, but there was no way to move without catching the other man's attention, either by sight or by noise.

"I cannot work under these conditions," Cardinal said passionately, shaking his head. He dropped the clump of hair onto the floor and hit his palm against the table. "I'm washing my hands of it!"

He stood, triumphantly, and caught sight of Alec for the first time.

Both men stood in silence for a long moment.

"Sir, I have the reports," Alec said finally. He held them out. This was not the right thing to do. He should have apologized and walked away, but his body seemed to be on autopilot. He felt himself walking across the floor to lay the papers on Cardinal's desk.

"*Fine.*" Cardinal snatched at them, then grabbed for his briefcase and shoved the papers inside. "But you'll have to wire them to me in New York moving forward."

"What?" Alec asked, confused. "New York?"

"I need to return to see to, ah…" Cardinal shook his head. "For health reasons," he said finally. He gave an emphatic nod. "Yes. The winters here are atrocious." He leaned forward over the desk to catch Alec's eye. "And, quite frankly, the bridge company is run by imbeciles! I'm fed up with every one of my decisions being questioned and with these, these—*laymen*—doubting my intellect!" He stood up and slapped the desk again before looking around for his coat. "I'm returning to New York."

"But who's going to supervise the construction?" Alec asked, bewildered.

Cardinal paused. From the look on his face, he hadn't thought that far ahead, and he tapped one foot on the floor as he thought.

Then his eyes focused on Alec. He gave Alec a once-over and nodded, businesslike.

"I need someone to stand in and keep things in line while I'm gone," he pronounced. "Someone whom I can trust. Someone who knows the value of hard work—and good work ethic! You have that, don't you...Alan?" He gave a winning smile.

"I do, sir, yes. But, it's...it's Alec." He wasn't sure the distinction mattered, given that the other man seemed to be having a psychotic break, but the words came out anyway.

"Yes, of course." Cardinal waved a hand. "That's what I said. Pay attention. Alec, I'm promoting you. While I am away, *you* will be site engineer."

"*What*?" Alec asked.

"I've seen your work," Cardinal said. He tapped on the desk and pointed a finger at Alec. "Yes. A real up-and-comer, aren't you? Started as a labourer. Worked your way up. I admire that. I've admired your technique, the way you...you keep your head down and get—things—done!" He punctuated the last three words with taps on the desk.

"Sir, I don't know what to say." Alec's mind was reeling.

Cardinal's eyes, which had been roving around the room, suddenly snapped over to focus on Alec's face.

"Don't know what to say?" Cardinal echoed, and his voice was falsely pleasant.

Alec swallowed. He had said the wrong thing and awoken the other man's fabled temper.

"It is simply…" He swallowed. "Well, with my current experience—"

"Do you realize what I'm offering you?" Cardinal asked, his voice still falsely pleasant. "You'll be doing far less for a great deal more in your take home pay. I think the words you're looking for are 'thank you.' Of course, if you don't *want* this opportunity—"

"Of course. Of course, I do." Alec tripped over the words. "Thank you, I'm incredibly grateful, sir. It is simply that—"

Cardinal cut him off with a wave and came to put a hand on Alec's shoulder. He was smiling once more, genial and winning. It would have been a chilling shift if he hadn't looked so unhinged.

"You know," he told Alec, as if it were a confidence, "I've always loved Sherlock Holmes."

"…Ah," Alec said lamely, at a loss for what to do with this new topic.

"His mind is a palace," Cardinal continued. He strolled to the window and stared out at the river, hands linked behind his back. "But, in every story, there is always the obstacle—those who doubt his vision. That is why Watson is so essential, you see."

He turned now, and waited for Alec to nod.

"Watson is the conductor of Holmes's intelligence," Cardinal explained. "He lets people know they can trust the mind of the great detective. Watson is the narrator, because it is with his voice that we can observe and come to trust Sherlock Holmes. That is what I need from you, Alec. I need you to be my voice, so that no more meddling can be done by those who lack vision."

He stared into Alec's eyes, and Alec tried to think what to say.

"Of course, if you don't want this responsibility…" Cardinal let the words hang in the air. "I'm sure I can find someone else."

"No!" Alec found his voice and nodded. "Sir, I am—I will do this. I can do this. Thank you. You have no idea what this means to me."

"Excellent," Cardinal said heartily. "This office is yours, then, Alec. Look around you, you are coming up in the world, yes?"

Alec managed to nod, and hoped he looked happier and more confident than bewildered and worried.

"Excellent." Cardinal strode to the door and grabbed his hat and his coat, then picked up his briefcase. "I will await your wires, Alec. Be my Watson." He nodded decisively and left without waiting for a response.

Alone in the room, Alec stared down at the desk, and then looked out at the river.

He could do this, he told himself. He would go through the blueprints line by line until he understood this structure as well as Cardinal did. He would learn the name of every crew leader. He knew engineering, and he knew work sites.

He could do this.

CHAPTER 20

Ben looked over at Esther. "I'm gonna go all *Star Wars* and say I have a bad feeling about this,"

"You and me both." Esther looked a bit worried. "Uh…I don't know about you, but I'm not sure I'm going to feel at all like having a party if we read any more."

"Well, you know what they say…" Ben looked back at the book. "That's the thing about making mistakes. Sometimes there's a luxurious amount of time before things go wrong."

"I hadn't heard that before." Esther looked intrigued.

"Of course, you haven't. You've never made a mistake in your life." Ben raised an eyebrow at her.

To his surprise, she looked stony-faced. "I make mistakes," she said, sounding wounded. "I just try my best, that's all. Why do you keep getting on my case about it?"

"It's funny?" Ben suggested.

She was, predictably, unamused by this. "It's *not*, though—and I've told you I don't like it and you keep doing it."

"I mean…that's how joking works between friends." Ben rolled his eyes. "Sorry if I hurt your—"

"Ben." It was like all of the anger had drained out of her. "Is that what your friends are like?"

Ben blinked at her. "…Yes?"

She considered this. "I'm sorry," she said finally.

He was going to ask her what she was sorry about, make a flippant joke, but the words stuck in his throat. Ben looked around for any sort of distraction…and his eyes landed on the deck of cards on his deck.

"Poker?" he suggested.

"Uh…sure." Esther closed the laptop and set it aside.

He tossed the pack of cards at her. "You play?"

"Eh." She looked embarrassed. "I can hold my own."

Ben smile and grabbed a chair. "This I gotta hear."

Ester pulled out the deck and started sifting through, removing jokers and the rule card. "You know when you're a teenager, and *no one* takes you seriously?"

"I still don't think anyone takes me seriously, but…sure."

She gave him a self-conscious sort of smile. "I was maybe 14 or so? Wasn't getting along with my parents. My grandmother was all up in my business about being ladylike, Yasmine was just a kid. I hated high school. I felt like I was too smart to waste my time on it, and like all of it was just pointless."

"Hey, something we agree on." Ben gave her a double thumbs up.

She gave him a smile that was equal parts amused and exasperated. "I said I used to feel that way, not like I still do. But, anyway, yeah. I discovered online poker. I was pretty good at it, too. You can account *exactly* for the odds, the uncertainty, all of it. It kind of taught me to accept that skill wasn't everything. But mostly…" She smiled a bit, "Mostly, it was just someone taking me seriously. Even if that someone was a bunch of adults with gambling issues."

Ben guffawed at that.

"Right?" She lifted one shoulder. "Maybe not the best group, in a way, but no one talked down to me. Everyone treated me like I was a real competitor. Even when they got angry and sent me awful messages, it was at least because of something I had *done*. And they didn't do that very often," she added hastily.

"So, you're in high school, you're…I don't know, emo, with the black clothes, and you're playing poker?"

"Did you see pictures of me in high school?" She looked suspicious. "Because that is eerily on the nose."

Ben guffawed. "Well, for what it's worth? If we met in high school, I would have thought you were pretty cool."

She blushed slightly under his regard and then raised an eyebrow and held up the deck of cards. "So. Do you want to fold now, or are you going to make me take the time to kick your ass?"

"O-ho." Ben was delighted. "Oh, I don't think it's going to go that easily for you, sunshine. I play to win. Come on, chips are in the common room."

He set out the chips on the coffee table and she flashed him a smile before beginning to shuffle the cards. "Five card draw, or Texas Hold Em?"

"Lady's choice."

She considered. "Five card draw."

Ben sat back in his chair and grinned as she shuffled a few times, not looking at the cards at all, and dealt them just as absent-mindedly. The movement was practiced, but not as smooth as he would have expected, and she smiled when she caught him looking.

"I played *online* poker," she reminded him.

"Ohhhhh. Right." Ben took his hand and hid a grimace. He had a queen, which wasn't terrible, but the rest were scattered low cards, no pairs or straights. He would have accused her of rigging the game, but he didn't want to tip her off to his bad hand.

Then he realized that if he said it slyly enough, she might think he was trying to bluff.

By then, however, he had missed the window.

He proceeded to learn two things: first, that Esther wasn't lying when she said she'd played a lot of poker; and second, that there was very little way to know how well a hand was going while it was still going on.

After his third surprise-loss, Ben pushed his cards back towards her and groaned. "How did I miss that one?"

"What did you discard?" Esther asked him as she reached out. She flipped over the cards in the discard pile and nodded contemplatively. "A flush was your best call. If you'd gotten what you needed, you'd have beaten me."

"And if I hadn't?" Ben said.

Esther smiled. "You still lost," she pointed out.

"Yeah, I remember." Ben's expression sharpened. She was throwing his loss in his face, and everyone knew that poker involved luck as much as skill. Just because she'd gotten better hands than he had didn't mean that she could really say she was better at this—

"Whoa." Esther put down the cards for a moment. "Do you want to stop playing?"

"Just deal," Ben said shortly.

She didn't. "Ben, I don't want this to…"

"To what?"

"To ruin what we have," Esther said quietly. She saw his surprised look and hastened to explain. "I know we haven't spent much time together, but I like spending time with you. I don't want to…lose that." She finished the sentence a bit lamely and raised one shoulder.

"You're not… I'm just frustrated." Ben shook his head.

"You reminded me a bit of Tyler, there. Getting all huffy."

"Hey. You don't know Tyler." He was surprised by how strongly his voice came out.

Esther sat back in her chair and frowned. "He annoys you. I see your face when he comes over to you drunk, or when he laughs in class. He's someone who doesn't want to take responsibility for his life."

"What does that mean?" Ben knew his voice was dangerous.

"He's not taking any of his classes seriously," Esther insisted. "He *reeked* of weed the other day in Ethics. I'm pretty sure he failed the midterm. And he's stopped even bringing a notebook or pencil to class in Materials. I'll bet he asks you to give him answers for homework, doesn't he?"

"You don't *know* him," Ben insisted. "You said all those things about me—or similar ones—and then admitted they were wrong. It's the same with Tyler. You don't know anything about him, you just assume things. And you don't like when people assume things about you, right? Like about an arranged marriage or stuff like that."

"That's different," Esther said heatedly. "*That's* people assuming that stereotypes fit me—"

"And you're assuming from what you know of Tyler that he doesn't care about school, and he doesn't want to take responsibility for his life," Ben snapped back. "That's a pretty big jump, don't you think?"

"Why are you even *defending* him?" She was shaking her head.

Ben opened his mouth, and there were too many memories to name all at once; the sheer volume of them choked him silent. He remembered his skinned knee and the aching in his throat while he hid under Tyler's back porch, frightened by the yelling in his own house, and Tyler crawling under to find him. *My parents fight, too. I hate it.* There was the millionth time Ben's father had called off picking him up at all, and Ben had taken a bottle of something from his mother's house—brandy? Whiskey? He couldn't remember anymore—and he and Tyler had drunk it out in one of the parks, hiding under the branches of a pine tree.

And there were dozens of others, hundreds of others, days when the two of them didn't need to talk at all because they knew exactly what the other person was going through. Even their fights were something Ben liked, if only for the novelty of it, the fact that he was actually exchanging words with Tyler, words that meant something, instead of icy silence and a string of insults, like there had been at home.

There was the way Tyler always understood what Ben meant, the way he tried to get Ben to come out of his shell. The way he'd kept Ben afloat when Ben thought the only two options were straight A's or flunking out.

"If you've never had a friend who always had your back," Ben said finally, "then I feel sorry for you."

She looked instantly hurt. "You assume just because I study, that I don't have any good friends?"

"That wasn't what I…meant." Although it sort of had been. "You've never needed a friend like Tyler, you didn't go through what we went through. You don't know what it's like not to be able to trust your own parents."

Esther frowned at that and put one foot up on the chair so she could rest her head on her knee. "And you really think Tyler has your back now, because he cares about you? He's not just using you?"

"Using me?" Ben raised an eyebrow.

"You're smart, Ben. Sometimes you just put two and two together in a way I'm so envious of, it all comes so naturally to you." She threw up her hands. "Are you telling me Tyler has never *once* tried to get you to cheat for him?"

He had been cooling down, but the fact that that
was true made Ben paradoxically furious.

"You don't know him," he said slowly and
precisely.

Esther took a deep breath, and then nodded.
"You're right, I don't."

Ben opened his mouth to continue the argument
before realizing it seemed to be over. "Wait, what?"

"You're right," Esther said. "I *don't* know Tyler.
You know him really well, and you say I'm wrong
about him. You know better than I do."

She seemed to be making an earnest attempt to
believe it, which almost made Ben feel guilty. After
all, she hadn't been wrong about all of it…

But that wasn't something he wanted to get into
now.

"Another hand?" Esther asked finally.

"Only if you tell me what you meant about taking
responsibility for my actions." Some part of him still
wanted a fight, and even though he knew he
shouldn't, he poked at the issue again.

Esther looked uncertain, but she licked her lips and
gave a little shrug. "Poker taught me a lot about
staying the course and doing the right thing, even
when the odds aren't all in your favor. You don't
always have a great hand, but you do have a best
course of action. It doesn't matter how much you
want to draw a specific card to finish your hand,
because the cards don't care. I made a *lot* of bad bets
at the start."

"You did?" Ben could not, for the life of him,
imagine her doing that.

"Oh, yeah. Absolutely. Ever heard of gambler's fallacy?" She began to deal.

"No."

"Basically, you start to get into the hole, and then you begin betting more on worse hands—because that's what you need to make up the deficit, and you tell yourself that it'll just…work out somehow." She shook her head with a smile. "It sounds ridiculous when you just say it, right? But you'd be surprised, it can really sneak up on you." She looked up and caught sight of Ben's expression. "What?"

"I…" He shook his head. "It's just weird hearing you talk about it."

"I know, I know. I don't fit the mold of the poker player with the cowboy hat and the stone-faced expression." She was smiling. "That was part of what was nice about playing online. My username was actually CowboyBlues."

Ben burst out laughing and handed over his cards for an exchange.

He didn't want to tell her, but that hadn't been the strange part of her monologue—at least, not as far as he was concerned.

What was strange was her sharing, so freely, the things she had not done well, and the traps her mind fell into. She spoke about her slip-ups and the times that things had gone wrong as if…there was nothing to be ashamed of.

She had even decided to keep doing something she wasn't great at because she could learn to be better, and she was *happy* when she talked about the traps she had fallen into, as if the traps were just fascinating quirks of the world.

He had never seen anyone talk about their weaknesses that way before—and he didn't know what to think about it now. He tried to imagine what his father would say, and shied away from that topic. His father had never once, to Ben's knowledge, admitted he was wrong about anything, much less delighted in it.

"Ben?"

He'd been staring off into the distance.

"Sorry," Ben said. "Uh…I bet 50."

There was the sound of laughter in the hall and Tyler flung the door open with carefree abandon. "Housekeeping! Want me to fluff your pillow?"

He had one arm slung around his date and the other came in shyly. When she saw Ben already sitting with another girl, her brow furrowed in confusion.

Ben cleared his throat uncomfortably and looked down at his hand. "Just my luck, the one hand I was going to do well on."

"We'll play again," Esther promised him. She began shuffling the cards while Tyler made a beeline for the fridge and pulled out some ciders.

"Thanks for grabbing booze, bro!" He nodded to Ben and cracked two of the ciders for the girls.

"You're welcome. And…Esther helped pay." Ben sat back in his chair.

"Oh. Cool." Tyler held up a cider. "I don't have any cash on me now, but remind me to pay you back later."

"Sure." Esther's expression was completely smooth, but Ben was fairly certain she knew the money was as good as gone.

CHAPTER 21

The apartment filled up quickly, with Tyler's room becoming the focal point for keg stands. A group played beer pong at a table near the door and music pounded from the stereo nearby.

With Esther's guidance, Ben had actually won a few hands of poker at this point. It was getting more difficult to focus with all the noise, however, and he kept seeing one of the girls come to stare at him balefully.

He hoped Esther hadn't noticed that.

He also hoped the people in his room weren't spilling too much booze on his stuff.

"Where's your bathroom?" Esther asked, as he shuffled the cards for another hand.

"Oh—the girls' bathroom is to the right out the door, at the end of the hallway." Ben looked over at her empty drink. "Another cider?"

"If there is one, sure. I think they all got taken." She was heading toward his room—to grab her bag, he assumed.

"I'll make you something, then—remember my skills in mixing drinks?"

"Nothing too strong," Esther warned him.

"Promise." Ben held up a hand in an oath-taking position, and then went to get some ingredients for a cocktail.

He stumbled when Tyler came out of nowhere at high speed. One arm snagged Ben into a head lock while the other hand rubbed on Ben's scalp. Ben yelped and threw an elbow, though Tyler was too drunk to do much more than grunt.

"*Finally*," Tyler said.

"Eh?" Ben bent to pick up the empty cider can, dropped in the struggle, and headed for the fridge.

"I thought she'd never leave." Tyler drained his beer and followed. "But don't worry, I am here to save your night. Beer pong! Now!"

"Nah." Ben sorted through the various liquors in the fridge and on the sideboard. "Where did the Schnapps go?"

"Drinking game." Tyler waved over at his room, where female laughter could still be heard. "Come on, man, Jess's friend is super hot—well, she's hotter than Esther—and she wants to get to know you. You've got an in…"

Ben, barely listening, was just giving up on any sort of drinkable cocktail when he spotted a lone cider in the back of the fridge. He grabbed it triumphantly, along with a can of beer, and stood up.

"I think I'm gonna walk Esther back to her place when she's ready," he told Tyler. "We've been having a good time playing, we'll just keep doing that." Though it had been getting difficult to hear, what with the crush of people.

An idea came to him: sneaking across campus to one of the fountains, to sit and drink and talk. The cards had been a good buffer, but Ben was beginning to think the buffer was getting in the way.

"Seriously?" Tyler looked after him.

"Apologize to Jess's friend for me," Ben called over his shoulder, as he headed for the hallway, drinks in hand.

In the bathroom, Esther emerged from the stall and began washing her hands. She could hear the music from the party even here, and she had never felt more out of place. Under the fluorescent lights, her face looked washed out and plain—and her hair, practical and simple, looked both unfashionable and unattractive. All the girls at the party had their hair up, and makeup on, and their clothes looked casual but weren't...

She fumbled in her bag, hoping she had some of Yasmine's makeup through some cosmic accident, but all she had was lip balm and sunscreen.

Esther groaned. All of the things she had so carefully cultivated about herself, the things she had been proud of, now seemed like a miscalculation.

But Ben had stayed and talked with her all night so far, never seeming to do so out of obligation, so maybe he really *did* like being with her. Esther sighed and dried her hands off. Then she tried a flirty smile in the mirror and tossed her hair.

No. She just looked ridiculous.

She heaved a sigh and bit both of her lips to bring more colour to them, then pinched her cheeks. She tried the smile again, and this time, it looked a little better.

Maybe she was getting somewhere.

Ben was loitering in the hallway, drinks in hand, when Tyler came out of the apartment. Tyler leaned against the wall and watched him for a while, until Ben sighed and looked over.

"*What*?"

"…Are you banging your partner?" Tyler sounded both horrified, and deeply amused.

"No," Ben said shortly.

"Ooooh, I saw that look. You *like* her."

"Dude, it's not like that—just give it a rest, okay?" Ben cast a worried glance at the bathroom door. If Esther heard Tyler rambling on, he could pretty much kiss his plans of a secluded drink goodbye.

"Uh-huh, so you normally spend a whole party playing poker with someone you have no intention of banging? Come on, man, this is me. Tell me—what's she like in bed?"

"Shut it," Ben hissed back, swinging to face Tyler. "I'm just trying to get to know her. She's cool!"

"I'm not angry, okay?" Tyler drew the words out, a faint slur on the end of them as he gestured. "After all, this is *good*, right? Yeah. If she's into you, you don't have to hack her computer anymore. She can just *give* us the assignments, right?"

"*Dude*." Ben grabbed at Tyler, who was now laughing drunkenly. "Shut *up*, what if she—"

But he heard a faint sound at the end of the hallway and turned to see Esther staring there, her eyes wide and hurt.

Tyler went silent with surprising speed.

"Esther." Ben reached for her, only to have her recoil. "Wait, listen. I wasn't—I would never do that to you. Never."

"I was just kidding," Tyler offered. He steadied himself on the wall and held up the other hand like he was swearing an oath. "Trust me. Ben is cool, he—"

"Dude, shut the fuck up," Ben hissed at him.

Tyler broke off, glaring.

"That's how you knew I aced the assignment," Esther said quietly. She was shaking her head now. "You hacked my laptop. You stole my *work*. Why?" The last word came out almost plaintively and she shut her mouth, pressing her lips together.

"Let me explain," Ben said desperately.

"And then you made it worse," Esther said. There were tears welling up in her eyes now, and he could tell she was furious about that. She wouldn't want to look emotional. "You were being all nice and…I don't get it, why would you make it *worse*?"

"Look." Ben edged forward. He couldn't hear Tyler anymore, which was good; at least the guy had enough sense to stay quiet. He got to Esther and put his hands on her shoulders, looking into her eyes. "Hey. I did some *dumb* shit before I met you, okay? I've done dumb shit for years. You saw the spray paint pictures, right?"

It was a weak attempt at a joke, but her lips twitched in answer.

"I don't want to be that guy anymore," Ben told her seriously.

Her eyes searched his and then she sighed, looked down—and his heart clenched.

"Just, please, *please*, don't get us expelled," Ben said desperately. "My dad would kill me."

Her eyes snapped open, and her expression went frigid. She batted Ben's hands off of her and shouldered her backpack before running for the exit.

"*Esther*!" Ben went to run after her, but a hand closed around his arm, and he was swung around.

"Just let her go," Tyler advised. Up close, his breath reeked of beer. "Come on, we'll—"

"Shut up." Ben tugged at his arm, his teeth bared. "This is all your fault."

"What?" Tyler spread his hands.

"You're always fucking things up," Ben spat at him.

Tyler's expression closed off. "I never forced you to do anything." He sounded a lot less drunk now. "Grow a pair."

Ben was moving before he had time to think about it. He shoved Tyler hard, and the other boy slammed against the wall of the corridor. In the apartment, there were shouts, but Ben didn't care. He advanced on Tyler as the door opened and their guests poured out into the hallway. The girls looked worried, but the guys were holding them back, waiting for Tyler and Ben to settle this themselves.

Tyler pushed himself off the wall and grabbed at Ben. They grappled for a moment before Tyler, always stronger, had Ben in a headlock. He leaned back, using the movement to create pressure on Ben's neck.

He wanted to make Ben tap out, lose in front of everyone, but the anger at that fact seemed very distant. All Ben had was the panic of being unable to breathe, and spots dancing in front of his eyes. He lashed out with his fists, hitting nothing the first couple of times, and then making solid contact. The pressure around his neck loosened.

When the spots cleared, Tyler was clutching his cheek, staring at Ben in betrayal. While Ben stood frozen, Tyler leapt at him, and his fist cracked across Ben's jaw. Ben felt a searing pain in his lip and then he was falling—

Now the other guys were going to get involved. They jumped in and pulled Ben and Tyler apart. Tyler, sliding into the crowd, was comforted by his date, and Ben looked up to see unfriendly expressions across the board.

He stared at them for a long moment, then shook his head and left, letting the door to the apartment slam behind him.

CHAPTER 22

A knock came at the door and Esther squeezed her eyes shut for a moment.

"Come in," she called, when her voice was steady.

She expected Yasmine or her mother, but it was her father who stooped under the doorway.

"Baba." Surprise distracted her. "What is it?"

"Just checking on you. You didn't eat breakfast."

"I ate up here." Esther braced for a fight.

Her father nodded his head to where her plate sat, with a single bite taken out of the bread, and the beans untouched. "It doesn't look like you ate at all."

"Oh." Her stomach *was* grumbling. Esther picked up the bowl of beans and began to eat mechanically. "Thanks for reminding me. Probably wasn't helping my focus any."

"Would you like to go get breakfast with me?" her father asked her. "Bring a cup of coffee to the park, maybe? We haven't seen much of you lately and it seems like…" He hesitated. "Well, it seemed like maybe you were a bit upset when you came in last night."

Esther froze. "You—I didn't think you were up when I came in." She frowned. "Were you just sitting in the dark in the living room, waiting for me? That's…" …*Creepy*, her brain finished.

"I was not." Now her father looked amused. "That said, when you're old enough to have children of your own, you will know that waiting to make sure they come home alright is hardly strange."

Esther tried to smile, but could not manage it. "I'll keep that in mind. How *did* you know, then?"

"A parent has their secrets," was all he said. "Are you well?"

She heaved a sigh and considered. By asking how he knew, she had inadvertently confirmed his suspicions. She normally wouldn't make a mistake like that, but she was tired. She hadn't slept well. She also supposed that she shouldn't consider honesty to be a mistake.

That would be thinking like Ben.

"I'm ready to be done with University," she said finally. "I don't belong there. I'll be glad when I can work with people who *care* about what they do, who have integrity. Sometimes I wish… I don't even know. I don't know what I would wish for."

Her father said nothing for a moment. Then, casually, he said, "Your mother mentioned you had an ethics assignment with a student you didn't really care for."

Esther gave him a look. He really was terrible when it came to subtlety.

"Yes," she told him. "And, it turns out, I was right not to care for him. I know he cheated on an assignment, and now, I just wish I knew the right thing to do. Do I turn him in?" She looked at her father uncertainly. "I'd have said that was the right thing to do, but I don't know anymore. Every time I think about doing it, I feel like…" Her chin trembled suddenly. "I feel like, *'this is why people don't like you.'*"

"*Azizam*." Her father came into the room at last and wrapped his arm around her where she was seated.

Esther pressed herself against his side and tried not to sniffle like a little child.

He let her regain her composure before he sat on the end of the bed and looked at her steadily. "Esther, when I was young, I was very much like you in some ways. I thought I always knew the right thing to do. Right and wrong, black and white. Yes? And if someone disappointed me, maybe I thought they were now a bad person."

"Baba, what he did—"

"Esther." His tone was strong, though not angry. "We are all flawed, yes? We try to be better, yes? And we fall short, all of us. What this boy did, it is not about you, *azizam*. It is about *him*. What you choose to do with your knowledge will be about *you*."

"If I do the wrong thing, though—"

"In time, you may think you made the wrong choice," he agreed, "and that is part of life, too. Do you think I have never looked back on choices and regretted them?"

Esther watched him silently. She did not know what to say, and she was worried that she would start crying if she tried to speak. As she watched, her father stood and touched her cheek briefly.

"Do not wait to make friends until you find perfect people," he told her softly. "And you tell me if you want to talk."

"I will." Esther swallowed and tried to keep her chin from wobbling. "Thank you, Baba."

When he was gone, she turned back to her desk and stared at the empty journal page in front of her. She had left Alec's journal in Ben's room, but she did not need Alec's words now. She needed her own. She picked up a pen, bit her lip, and began to write. Hopefully, with the words, would come clarity.

Ben pushed the door open and had the vague impression of Tyler on the couch and a level of Mario Kart running on the TV. Ben hesitated. He didn't want to speak to Tyler, and he definitely didn't want to see the bruise he'd given his friend, but perhaps he needed to. Perhaps he should apologize—

Tyler continued to play, though the set of his chin said that he had definitely noticed Ben's entrance, and when he got to a straightaway, he tossed a look in Ben's direction.

"She dump you yet or did you get her to stay by telling her you've *changed*?" Mockery dripped through every word.

Ben shook his head and walked into his room. The door closed harder than it should have, though it wasn't the slam he really wanted. He should have known better than to expect anything else of Tyler. Not a call, not a text, no apology of any kind, and here was Tyler continuing to insist that Ben and

Esther had been something more than friends, and
that Ben was solely to blame for Esther's reaction the
other night.

When *Tyler* was the one who had spilled the
beans.

Ben gave a groan and flopped back on his bed to
stare at the ceiling. Esther hadn't responded to his
text, and she hadn't picked up when he called, either.
He had spent the night—and early morning—walking
around the neighbourhood, sneaking across campus
so that he could avoid the security guards who would
tell him to go back to his apartment and go to sleep.

He hated this. He hated the sanctimonious way
Esther had judged him when they first met, the way
she had just jumped to the wrong conclusion when
she heard about the cheating. It wasn't as if he had
meant to make it worse. He had actually liked
hanging out with her, why couldn't she see that?

And now she might turn him in. He sat up and
went to his computer. He drummed his fingers on the
desk while it booted up and tried to contain his
impatience. When it was finally awake, he deleted the
files. It would be possible for someone to find them
again, if they knew what they were doing, but they
likely wouldn't.

Without any evidence, it would be her word
against his, and that wouldn't be enough to get him
expelled.

Probably.

His eyes fell on the journal, and he shoved it off
the bed and onto the floor before burying his face in
his hands. He was exhausted. He wanted to sleep, but
anxiety kept gnawing at him. He hated this place. He

hated the teachers making little puzzles for all of the students to figure out, like they were rats in a maze. He hated his mother treating him like a child who couldn't even buy food for himself. He hated his father, pretending he was so much better than everyone else because *he* was an engineer.

Well, soon I'm going to be an engineer, too. What now?

Or...he was, if Esther didn't turn him in.

Ben dropped his hands and hunched his shoulders as the victory sound played from the main room. He was now angry, on top of everything, that Tyler was playing video games instead of freaking out like Ben was.

But the anger didn't last long. Its comforting warmth disappeared all too soon, leaving Ben with nothing more than the cold drip of worry.

He had to get out of this. He had to find some way to make sure Esther wouldn't tell, and that meant he had to find something she wanted. His eyes scanned the room and landed on the journal, now on the floor. If he found something good enough in there...

It was as good an idea as any.

CHAPTER 23

Ginette took Alec's hand to get down from the carriage. With one hand clasped protectively over the swell of her belly, she was focusing more on where she was stepping than on the façade of the house. Of course, she had seen it every day—she would not think to look up at the siding, which was new and fresh. He thought she might at least notice the new front steps beneath her feet, but she was exhausted, as she so often was these days, and she only leaned against him as they came into the house.

To this day, he could not stop the leap of awe every time she touched him. When she smiled at him, he felt he could move mountains and part seas, anything to make her happy.

Hopefully, the house would be a start.

Indeed, she stopped suddenly when she saw the interior, her mouth opening in a little O of surprise. He saw her eyes trace over the familiar placement of the windows, trying to determine if this was, indeed, their house.

It was. He looked around and felt a great weight lifted from him, shame gone after months of having it around his neck like a millstone. Every time he came to this house, he had seen only his failure to provide for Ginette.

Now, though… Now there was new paint on the walls, the smell still fading. All of the drafty, old sills had been replaced and the cracks in the walls were gone. The floor was freshly laid down, with their old, battered table replaced. Through the bedroom door, it was possible to see the glint of a new brass bed.

"Alec," Ginette breathed. "That's—it's not just the new paint. Those curtains are new! The table. A new kettle, even." She gave a wondering laugh. She had struggled with the old, dented kettle nearly every day. She looked up at him and her eyes were shining.

"Do you like it?" He smiled down at her.

"*Like* it?" She gave an uncertain laugh, and he saw worry in her eyes all of a sudden. "I…am trying to wrap my head around how we can *afford* it."

"I've been promoted." Alec drew her to a new, comfortable chair by the wood stove. He knelt by the chair as she settled into it. "Mr. Cardinal returned to New York and, based on the work I had been doing, he promoted me to site engineer while he's abroad."

"Oh, Alec!" She could not stop herself from smiling, but the confusion was still there. "But—"

"Tell me what you think of the colour," Alec prompted her. He reached out to brush his fingers over the new paint. "If you don't like it, we can have it redone." *There's no need to worry,* he wanted to say. *Everything will be as it should be now.*

She smiled and leaned forward to kiss him. "It's perfect," she said earnestly. "Truly, Alec."

He saw the worry return to her eyes and bit his lip.

"Alec…" Ginette was fiddling with her ring. "Something about this doesn't feel right to me."

"Don't worry." Alec reached out to clasp her hands. He held her gaze. "I work directly below Mr. Cardinal now. I see each of the blueprints, each of the reports. If something is wrong, I will be the first to know."

Ginette swallowed. She bit her lip, a mirror of him, and then she said, in a rush: "It seems too quick for you to be given that level of responsibility. You've only been apprenticing a short time and—"

"Of all the people to doubt me." The words seemed to come out on their own. Alec's mouth tasted bitter with it.

"It's not that!" Ginette protested.

"No?" He wanted to turn away. He could not listen to this. "You always told me to speak up for myself. Would you prefer I had turned this down instead?"

"No! No." She shook her head. "No, Alec."

"So be *happy* for me." This was not how he had imagined this moment. He had thought she would be glad. "Be happy for us, Ginette. This is a good thing!" Alec swept his hand around him to take in the paint, the curtains, the furniture.

There was a pause, and he held his breath, but then Ginette ducked her head and nodded.

"Of course." When she looked up, she was smiling. "Yes, Alec. I only want what's best for you."

"For us," Alec said again. He leaned forward to kiss her and felt her melt under his touch. "Come. I want to show you the rest of the house."

She rose awkwardly, her belly overlarge next to her tiny frame, and she followed him to the sink, fitted with new pipes, the window set with new panes. She smiled and set the stove to heat water while they explored the rest of their new house.

In the bedroom, she stopped and covered her mouth at the sight of a beautiful armoire. "Alec, oh, you didn't. This work…" She turned to him. "Did you make it?"

"Oh, no." The thought of himself, labouring away in a workshop like a tradesman, was almost abhorrent to him. "I bought it downtown. Such a fine make."

"Not as fine as you could have made," Ginette said, almost stubbornly. "Alec, I loved all of the pieces you made for us." She looked around. "Where…where is the trunk you made me?"

"Replaced." He could barely contain his joy. He went to the new one, leather banded, and showed her how smoothly it opened. "Isn't it beautiful, Ginette? See the tooling on the leather. I could never have done that for you."

"I…see." She gave a smile and sat on the bed.

"Are you well?"

"Just…very tired." She looked drawn now.

"I'll make you a meal," Alec told her. "Well…something, at any rate. You rest here, my love, in your new bed. I am so glad to show you all of this. I hope you're happy."

"Oh. Oh, yes." She gave him a smile. "Of course I am, Alec. I am glad of this house, and glad of your promotion, too."

He smiled and ducked out of the room. Something seemed strange about her manner, but all he could think was that she would soon see how much this was worth. She had *said* she was content with her life, but

she had always known better before she married him.
She would be glad to tell her friends that she had
married a worthy man, surely.

His gaze swept around the house and came to rest,
at last, on his briefcase. He had been so consumed
with the thoughts of a new house, that he had not
thought to get new clothing and a new briefcase.
And…he looked down and grimaced at his shoes. He
must get new shoes, as well.

Soon, they would leave this place behind entirely.
He leaned against the counter and looked at the door.
Outside there was mud and misery, families under
leaky roofs, children going hungry. It was a life he
had accepted for himself, but he would be damned if
he let Ginette live it—or their children.

The water was still heating for tea, and he went
quietly to the door to look in at her. She had fallen
asleep on the bed with her eyes shadowed from
exhaustion. She had lost weight while she was in the
hospital, and she'd had little to lose. The arch of her
belly moved, however; the child turning, settling to
sleep with her.

Alec crept closer to her and laid a kiss on her
forehead gently.

"I will always take care of you, my love," he
whispered. He smoothed the hair from her sleeping
face and smiled down at her, and then felt something
catch in his pocket.

The hospital bills. He stood quickly and left before
Ginette could wake and catch sight of his face. The
pink slips of paper held numbers that made him quail,
but he told himself that he had a good job now. He
was rising. He would have the money to pay these

bills, to buy Ginette a new house in a good part of town.

He would do anything for her.

Ben paused, looking down at the page. Though Alec had written of the pressures of money and ambition, surely something that resonated across the ages, Ben could think only of Alec's words to Ginette: *Of all the people to doubt me.*

That had cut deeper to him than any of the rest of it. The fear that he would not measure up, that he did not know what he was doing—that was nothing to Ben. It was a game. He played it every day to see if he could "win" at school while doing the least work possible.

But the doubt of someone Alec had pledged his life to, that cut him to the bone. He laid the book down for a moment and struggled to gain his breath. When you got older, when you were established, no one should question you. No one should question an engineer. That was the rule.

That was how it worked.

Wasn't it?

CHAPTER 24

The entries continued with surprising regularity, enough that Ben wondered if Alec brought the journal to work with him. The progress of the bridge had been sketched out, showing the rapid progress as the cantilevered design was fleshed out. Alec's drafting hand was good, keeping strict proportions to the drawing despite the fact that the sketch had been done quickly.

He'd had a good mind for his work, Ben thought. There were some pages about grumbles from the day labourers, and Ralph's continued contempt for Alec. Ben felt his lip curl every time he read the other man's name; as with Ginette, the disrespect for Alec hit him viscerally. Alec was rising in the world, using every means at his disposal to do better for his family.

But some people were quick to tear down anyone above them. Ben's father had said that more than once when someone got in his way. Some people were just better at playing the game than other people were, or they had a better hand dealt to them. It wasn't fair, and you couldn't try to play the game fairly, or you'd get trampled.

Alec had only done what he needed to do.

Ben flipped through the entries about the bridge. If he flipped the pages quickly enough, he could make a time-lapse drawing of sorts, like something out of a historical film. Alec had brought the project back to schedule, it appeared—though Cardinal never seemed to be satisfied. His messages from New York were infrequent. Alec contacted him often, only to hear silence for weeks and then a brusque admonition on some aspect of progress.

Alec was careful in how he spoke of Cardinal, even in his private journal. His entries became far less textured with observations and emotions when he spoke of his boss, small paragraphs stripped down to the facts and nothing more.

Without Alec's personal observations, Ben was left to form his own—and he did, quite strongly. He had seen people walk away from projects before, washing their hands of the process while it was still ongoing. Cardinal wanted to be done with this bridge, he wished he had never taken on the project. He would engage with it only rarely, and then under duress.

But Alec had more to focus on than simply Cardinal. He wrote of the Kahnawake steelworkers and the board of directors, of Jean's worries and the loss of some workers to other building projects. He also wrote extensively about Ginette, about the way she was still unsettled in their nicer house, how the neighbours treated them differently now—and how Ginette was finding everything more difficult as she came close to giving birth.

By the time Alec wrote an account of the birth, itself, his writing was unsteady and Ben could almost

feel the sleep deprivation oozing from the words. Luc
had arrived at night, after a long and difficult birth,
but Ginette had never complained of the pain or the
exhaustion; Alec wrote, awestruck, of how she had
persevered, and had held out her arms at once for her
son.

*In the hospital, with one arm around her shoulders
and the other cradling my son, I felt a sense of being
entirely complete,* Alec had written. *He is little yet,
but he has a strong grip and a stronger cry—and his
eyes are as blue as the sky. He is perfect.*

There were surprisingly modern-sounding
mentions of having in-laws underfoot and his mother-
in-law, especially, around the house each day, as well
as being up well into the night when the baby cried.
He mentioned singing his grandmother's old lullabies
to the baby, and he wrote proudly that he had seen the
baby's first smile but had not wanted to distress
Ginette by telling her.

As things went better at home, they seemed to go
worse on the job. Jean and the workers had continued
worries about safety precautions, and—in the absence
of any response from Cardinal—Alec was left to
reassure them on his own. It wasn't long before a
faction, headed by Ralph, held a strike and then
walked off the job. Others came back, unwilling to
risk their paycheck, but the damage was done. The
mood on the job site became sullen and tinged with
bad memories.

The board didn't seem to care, Alec reported. They
had hardly entertained a single meeting about the
strike, and they had instructed him to hire new
workers rather than appease the others. His warnings

about working conditions fell on deaf ears; the budget was tight, they told him, and there was no slack for more materials or for "softer" conditions. The workers could leave if they did not like it, and only a few would dare do so, which—to the board—meant that the problem was solved.

Alec was deeply distressed to realize that this was, in fact, true. He spoke of this topic carefully as well, though Ben sensed it was more to protect his own feelings than anything else. Alec had been in the same shoes as those workers not so long ago, and he felt the harsh conditions keenly.

The machine ground on, however, not caring for a lone engineer—even the site manager—who might have misgivings. After the first burst of activity, progress slowed to small and not-readily-visible aspects of the construction, so that Alec was often sharing pictures of small components that shored up the struts, or additions to the pylons.

In short order, Alec found a new house for his family. He wrote proudly about the house, about how well it was constructed, how solid—and he did work himself to fix up the little things that others might not have been able to. Ben sensed that Alec still enjoyed working with his hands. Taking time to shore up a porch was altogether simpler than the politics of the job site.

And politics, there were. He might be moving up in the world in most ways, but there were a great many other engineers at the job site who did not appreciate Alec's sudden rise. He wrote that he did not want to trouble Ginette with the details, and so all of them were poured into his journal, ranging from

exhaustive lists of insults, and terse entries: *Tout de
meme aujourd'hui.*

Ben understood why Alec was not sharing the
details with Ginette. She worried enough about
expenses as it was. For all that she had been raised in
comfort, she found ways to save pennies now. She
argued with Alec when he wanted to bring in a maid
to do the cleaning and cooking—*my heart, I am
perfectly capable*—and Alec was open in the journal
about his confusion.

Sometimes, Ben wondered if Ginette's gift had not
made Alec more forthcoming with his words, but
instead, more secretive.

It was not all frustration, at any rate. Both Alec
and Ginette delighted in Luc, and there were
mentions of idyllic days beside the river, or pushing
Luc on a swing, teaching him to take his first steps.
Both Alec and Ginette, it seemed, had shed some
tears when Luc was old enough to move to his own
room with the nursemaid. Alec described waking in
the night and easing his way out of bed to check on
Luc without waking Ginette...only to find her already
by Luc's door, peering into the darkness and listening
for the sound of her son's breathing.

With the two of them so enchanted by Luc and by
each other, Ben was surprised that it took as long as it
did for Ginette to conceive again. By the time she was
afflicted with morning sickness, the construction was,
once again, leaping ahead.

Alec mentioned McDougall briefly, and Ben could
almost feel the guilt coming off the page—as well as
relief, for McDougall had secured a contract as a
consulting engineer with the government. It seemed

that his fortunes had recovered after he had been let go by Cardinal. Alec mentioned that he sometimes wished to write to McDougall, but it seemed that he did not dare, especially after taking the other man's place.

The months crept by, from a dark winter and into a cool spring. The flowers came late, as did summer, but the heat descended with a vengeance. Ginette's last weeks were so miserable that she accepted Alec's choice to get yet another maid. She was often asleep by the time he arrived home in the evenings, sometimes with Luc curled up by her side, and in midsummer, she gave birth to another boy, Etienne.

They were perfect days, and something about them meant that Ben did not look away even though this brought him no closer to understanding what had happened at the bridge. Even as Alec struggled at work, enduring the back talk and arguments with the other engineers, what he had with Ginette was almost achingly perfect.

Ben had not imagined marriage much, but his parents' relationship had hardly given him confidence in the concept. Alec and Ginette, however, had something that Ben had never seen before. He read Alec's reflections of Luc falling asleep, or of seeing Ginette smiling on a beautiful day, and there was something there...

His phone buzzed somewhere, and Ben gave a look around the room. It was still charging, and the break had made him aware that his shoulder was aching. He had been leaning on it as he read and now he sat up to continue.

There was an ominous ring, after all, to the sentence, Jean is worried, as am I. There has been an incident.

CHAPTER 25

Alec was almost to the job site when he heard the groan. At first, he thought it must be an animal nearby, but no animal would be so loud. It sounded at once haunting and earthy, and he stopped to consider. He was not the only one tilting his head, trying to determine where it was coming from.

The bridge. Alec went cold. He hardly breathed as he waited for the rest of what must surely be coming: the crashes, the screams. When none of those sounds followed, and not even another groan, he broke out in a sweat and wiped a trembling hand over his brow.

He was being ridiculous. The sound had come from a nearby house or shop, it was nothing.

He was so relieved, he felt as if he were floating by the time he reached the job site. There was a knot of steel workers clustered around someone—Jean, Alec guessed—and all of them were peering at the same thing, jostling for a look.

They parted when they saw Alec and he noticed their worry. It had been Jean they were clustered around, and he looked graver than Alec had ever seen him, blueprints held out in front of him.

"Jean," Alec called. "*Ca va*?"

Jean did not smile; his lips did not even twitch. He held out the blueprints and hesitated briefly when Alec came to his side. Then he sighed and turned the blueprints to see them.

They were marked, as Alec's grandmother would have said, seven ways to Sunday. Measurements were crossed off and replaced in a rough hand.

"What is this?" Alec asked. "These measurements are way off." He wasn't able to do all of the calculations in his head, but they were outside the realm of what he would consider feasible.

"They *are* way off." Jean tapped the blueprint. "They're also *accurate*."

"What d'you mean?" Alec looked at him blankly. The moment the words were out of his mouth, he could have cursed himself. His cheeks were heating, and the very silence around them felt like a crushing weight. They were all listening to him, the site engineer, as the foreman explained something on the blueprints.

Shame made it difficult to make anything out beyond the ringing in his ears, and he had to force himself to focus on Jean.

"I mean..." Jean turned to sweep one hand at the bridge. "The measurements I wrote here on the paper are the actual measurements."

"Wait." Alec looked at him, then at the other steelworkers. They were watching him with interest, almost as it—

They thought he had done it. His chest felt cold.

He took a deep breath and held out a hand to Jean. "Slow down. You're telling me that the measurements on the blueprints do not match the measurements...of the bridge? How is that possible?"

"Yes," Jean said. He was speaking as if to a small child. "We've followed our instructions for connecting each support, but some of the struts appear to be bending. Today, the structure made a...noise."

"A noise?" Alec echoed.

Jean said nothing for a moment.

"I need to know what kind of noise," Alec started to say, and Jean cut him off wearily.

"I have never heard anything like it before," he told Alec bluntly. "It sounded like the Earth was opening beneath me. I'm no engineer, Alec, but something is definitely wrong here."

Alec looked down at the blueprints. His mind was racing. He did not look over to the bridge; he did not want to see that Jean was correct. If, he told himself. If Jean was correct.

"This is the first I'm hearing about this," he said carefully. He reached over to take the blueprints, and he examined it more closely before looking up. "Are you not following the design specifications?"

Jean's eyes flashed. "Alec. Do you really think I would jeopardize the integrity of the site?" Some workers murmured in agreement, and he held out a hand when their voices began to rise. All the while, he held Alec's eyes. "I'm not trying to get anyone killed. Answer me honestly, Alec—are you sure about this design? The beams are supporting a lot of weight, and they're far, far out from the pier."

Alec looked down at the blueprints once more. His head was racing, and he could feel the others watching them. Jean waved them back before laying a hand on Alec's shoulder.

"You're the site engineer," Jean told him quietly. "We're counting on you."

That gave Alec the strength to nod. He took a deep breath. "I'll inform Mr. Cardinal about this right away. Let's hold off for now, and I'm sure it will all be cleared up in no time." He nodded around at the group of workers, whose faces eased.

Drafting the letter took longer than he liked, but Alec was done by midmorning, in time for the boy from the post office to take the letter back. Then he sat and stared out at the job site. Work had slowed to a crawl, there being little to do until they were cleared to go back onto the bridge, and Jean was watching all of it with his arms crossed, staring at the massive structure. Even from hundreds of yards away, Alec could pick him out—and see the tension in him.

It would be okay, he told himself. Cardinal would be back in touch soon. Of all messages, he surely would not ignore *this* one.

The phone buzzed again as Ben flipped the page. There were no more entries. He skipped ahead, and still found nothing.

The hair on the back of his neck rose.

Another buzz, and he went to check his email. There were a series of three from the graduation committee, reminding them to put down a deposit for caps and gowns, make sure their transcripts were accurate, and have their apartment rooms cleaned by the last day of senior week. Ben rolled his eyes and scrolled through. He hadn't had any interest in those things a few days ago, and he certainly didn't now. In fact—

He stopped dead, staring at his phone.

There was another email, one from Professor McLeary, telling Ben to be at a meeting at his office in three hours. It wasn't a request, there was no mention of what time would work for Ben—just the time and the location.

She'd done it. Esther had actually turned him in. Ice-cold dread turned into rage and Ben fought the urge to throw his phone across the room. How the fuck *dare* she? Who was she to pretend that she was so wonderful? She was some teacher's dream student, she was little miss perfect, but that didn't make her better than him, it didn't mean that everyone else in the world should have to live their life the way she did, without any fun at all.

That. Bitch.

Ben strode across the room and picked up the journal and one of the books Esther had left behind. *Fine*. He would give these back to her. He'd make sure she looked him in the eyes when he gave those back. He'd go over to her house after seeing McLeary and he'd—

Wait. What if she was there?

She wouldn't be there. He rolled his eyes and tried to stuff both books into his bag, only to drop one on the floor. When he went to pick it up, however, he slumped onto the bed and dropped his head into his hands. To his horror, he felt the prickle of tears in his eyes.

What the hell was going to happen to him? He hadn't been lying when he said his father would go ballistic. The man had always viewed Ben's university fees as a waste, saying—loudly—that Ben should find his own path in life. Now…he'd not only be right, he'd be out thousands of dollars, and he was going to be furious.

And Ben's mother would…just be disappointed. She'd want to talk about it. She'd try to have Ben talk to Steve about it. He would almost rather just be yelled at by his father.

He picked up the book and flipped it over: The Quebec River Bridge Disaster, with a suitably boring picture of the bridge. Ben flipped through it. There were pictures of steel workers, one of Teddy Cardinal looking like a giant asshole—though oddly familiar—and then…

Ben blinked down at the picture. He had the sense that this wasn't real. He had seen that picture before. Slowly, he turned his head over to the collage of photos on the wall, and then got up on his bed, shoes and all, to look between his wall and the book.

"Holy…" He gave a last few looks, as if either one of the pictures might disappear at any moment.

But they didn't.

"Son of a *bitch*."

CHAPTER 26

B en locked his bike up in front of the engineering building more out of habit than anything else. No one was going to want to steal it. Before today, it had already been on its last legs, and that was before he'd ridden it onto campus at well over any speed it should go.

Ben limped down the hallway and tried to calm his racing heart. This was going to suck, but he could barely focus on it at all. The only thing he could think about was the picture in his backpack. Esther had to see it—

Esther wouldn't want to see it. Esther was here to turn him in. That thought came with a flush of shame and anger that he pushed out of the way. What was going to happen, would happen, he told himself. He deserved this. If he didn't want to be the person Esther had justifiably accused him of being, he needed to be someone else—someone who would walk into the professor's office and take the consequences of what he had done.

He stopped in front of the door that said PROFESSOR S. MCLEARY in gold typeface and looked up to see none other than Esther, herself, coming down the hallway. Her face was drawn, and her back was rigid. She looked, strangely, like she was dreading this. As if, in her own way, she was dreading this just as much as he was. There was a flicker of the desire to talk her out of it and he grimaced to himself.

No. He was going to take responsibility.

"Esther." He swung his bag off his back.

"Let's just go in." She didn't look at him.

"Wait. I want to show you something."

"Ben, I have no interest in—" She stopped when she saw the book in his hands. "Oh. I...thank you. I forgot I left that."

"It's—there's something in here." Ben flipped open to the relevant page and held it out to her. "Look."

"Professor McLeary is waiting for us," she told him impatiently.

"This'll just take a second. Look. Look at the caption. That's Teddy Cardinal. Short for Theodore Cardinal...and his wife."

Esther sighed as she took the book. "Yes. I've seen this picture."

"Where?" Ben asked her. "Where did you see it?"

"In...this book?" She shook her head.

"Did you?" Ben asked her. He held out the photo he had used to mark the page. "Or did you see it on my wall? Did you see the picture I had found of my Great Grandma Lillian...and my Great Grandpa Theo?"

"Wait." Esther gaped at him before taking the picture. "Wait. This is the same picture. I mean, I know it is, I just—wait. Did you know this the whole time? What were you—"

"Nope." He shook his head and held up his hands. "Honest to God, Esther, I didn't. I just found out today. I mean, just now. I…anyway, I thought…you might be interested. I thought you'd want to see."

She looked up at him suspiciously.

"Let's go in," Ben told her.

Now her eyes narrowed. She looked down at the photo for a moment. "So…you come from a long line of engineers?" She repeated his words from days ago, and she didn't look up at him.

"I don't—" Ben swallowed convulsively. "I literally learned about this an hour ago and I've been really trying not to think about that. Let's just say I have a much better picture of Theodore Cardinal in my head now." He looked up from the photo to see her staring at him. "What?"

"I…nothing." She shook her head and looked at the photo once more before handing it back to him. "Thanks for showing me."

"Let's go in," he said again.

"Really? You're not taking this like I expected you would—"

"I'm serious." He blew out a breath and shoved his hands in his pockets. "I know we have to, but I'd rather get it over with, if you don't mind. Not really looking forward to it." He raised his hand and rapped on the door before he could think better of it.

"Come in!" Professor McLeary called. Classical music turned off abruptly.

Ben opened the door and nodded to his professor. "Hello. We're both here."

McLeary gave him a professional nod. "Take a seat, then, both of you."

"Yes, sir." Ben sat, his palms suddenly clammy. He was intensely aware of Esther's presence at his side. When he stole a glance, she was staring down at her lap, frowning.

"Thank you for coming in," McLeary told Ben formally, drawing Ben's attention back to him. "Esther said this was very important, but said it was not something to discuss in an email. Esther?"

Ben swallowed. *If you want to be someone different, then be someone different.* He raised his chin and looked over at her, giving a tiny nod. "Go ahead."

"There was a…problem…with the project." Esther wasn't looking at him.

Professor McLeary waited in silence for a few moments before annoyance flitted across his face. He seemed to tamp it down quickly. "Would you care to elabourate?" he asked, with a shade too much courtesy.

"She shouldn't have to," Ben found himself saying. He could feel part of himself screaming to shut up because this was the stupidest thing he'd ever done. He kept talking, though, whether from blind courage or utter stupidity, he wasn't sure. "It was my fault," he told Professor McLeary. "Esther had great ideas for the project, she did a lot of good work, and then a couple of days ago, she found out—"

"That he can't be objective about the material," Esther broke in.

Ben choked and pounded himself on the chest.

"Ben's great grandfather was Theodore Cardinal," Esther explained.

Professor McLeary's eyebrows shot up. When Esther handed over the book and the picture, he stared between them in consternation.

"O'Betany," he murmured. "I admit, I hadn't made the connection."

"So, it wasn't working. We couldn't see eye to eye. I'd like to present separately." Esther had the good sense to shut her mouth instead of making up an elabourate lie.

Professor McLeary took another look at the photo and the book, then handed them back to Esther, who gave Ben the picture.

"Well, then," McLeary said finally. "This is certainly an unusual situation, but as long as you both understand what needs to be done, I don't think there's anything else we need to discuss. The paper submission date remains the same, but you two will be given separate presentation slots. Mr. O'Betany, I see no reason you should have to mention your family connection if you don't want to."

"Thank you, professor." Esther said. She gave a mechanical smile.

"Well, then, since we're all agreed." Professor McLeary nodded to them both and turned back to his computer in what was a polite, but unmistakable, dismissal.

Esther grabbed her bag and headed out the door, sliding easily past Ben while he sat frozen and tried to figure out what had happened. A second later, however, he was fumbling for his phone and following her. He barreled out the door and looked around frantically, only to see her half-running for the door.

"Esther!" Ben called.

She didn't stop walking, didn't even slow down.

"Esther! *Esther*." He sprinted after her and grabbed at her arm. She pulled it out of his grasp without looking at him, and so he scrambled to stand in front of her.

Her eyes flashed. "Do you mind?"

"Can you please just talk to me?" Ben asked her.

"What's left to say?" she challenged him.

"You…you didn't say anything about…" Ben gestured back towards Professor McLeary's office.

Esther waited for him to speak, and when he did not, her expression turned sharp. "About what? Academic dishonesty? Invading my privacy? Jeopardizing my career?"

Ben swallowed.

"I need to go." She pushed her way past him.

"Wait," Ben begged her. "Why? Why did you do that? Why let me off the hook?"

"What do you *care*?" She wheeled around then, and he saw that her chin was trembling again. "You got what you wanted, right?" She dashed a hand across her eyes.

"This isn't what I wanted." Ben put his hands out. Everything in his head was a muddle except this. When he saw Esther crying, he knew for certain that he hadn't wanted things to happen like this. "I mean it. I never wanted this."

For a moment, she looked hopeful, and then her expression hardened again. "Then go back in there and tell him the truth."

Ben froze. He'd gotten out of this. She'd decided not to turn him in.

But she was right. He took a deep breath and nodded. "Fine."

She sighed and pressed her lips together. "Don't. Consider this a freebie."

"What? Why?"

"The world needs people who can own up," Esther told him. "I don't know what happened between the last time we talked and now, but…you've changed." She cleared her throat. "Anyway, I'm gonna go. I…look forward to seeing your presentation."

"Hey." Ben pulled out the journal. "It doesn't go all the way to the end, but there's some interesting stuff."

She hesitated. "There are some first-hand accounts in the library," she told him. Her face was studiously blank. "From the day of the collapse. Jesse—the reference librarian—she'll help you find them."

Ben nodded and purposefully didn't watch her as she left. He was feeling weak now, in the aftermath of the adrenaline. He had to know what had happened to Alec, however, and so he set off with tottering steps to Thode library, to find the aforementioned Jesse.

Within half an hour, he was sitting at one of the desks, poring through the documents.

CHAPTER 27

Jean was waiting when Alec came down the hill from the office.

"Any word?" Jean called.

Alec shook his head. "None specifically. There was another message from him by telegram, but nothing regarding the report."

Jean shook his head. "No response isn't confirmation."

Alec put his hands in his pockets and tried to slow his heartbeat. The board had been clear what they thought of the delay, and without any further noises from the bridge… "Jean…we're behind schedule."

Jean looked over at him incredulously.

"Mr. Cardinal would surely have seen the reports by now. We need to resume construction and get things back on track. The south end is ready."

"No."

"We open next *month*, Jean."

"No." Jean shook his head. "I don't trust that man."

Alec gave a nod. "You don't have to, though. Trust me. Just trust me, Jean." He reached out to clasp the other man's shoulder. "Ncwatsíńen, right?"

"Ncwatsíńen." Jean's face relaxed. "All right, Alec." He turned and gave a sharp whistle, waving to the crew. "*Allons-y!*"

Theodore Cardinal struck a match and lifted it to the pipe in his mouth. The tremor in his hands was worse than usual today, and it took three tries and another match to light the damned thing. He swore and shook out his fingers before running the same hand through his hair and sitting back in his leather office chair.

The day's mail was still sitting, unopened, on the desk in front of him. One envelope had the return address of a small town in Iowa, a town that could not remotely pay his rates, while another showed Quebec City's return address. He should hand that over to Myrtle; he had no interest in wading through the same, tiresome requests over and over again.

That damned bridge was the last thing he wanted to think about.

Once—years ago, now—the first puff from his pipe would put him into a state of jovial contentedness. It was a civilized ritual, the sort of half-physical thing you could do with your mind elsewhere, and toast to the success of the day while you took a short break.

Then those short breaks had become ever more frequent as the trembling in his hands had increased. At first, a few puffs were all it took to calm himself, but now it seemed that he took as much time smoking as he did working.

There wasn't any choice in the matter. He couldn't have shaking hands. He was an engineer. His lines had to be precise. He had been making some of the interns do his blueprints for months, and he thought they were beginning to suspect—

"Excuse me, Sir." The door had opened and Myrtle stood there, hair back in that too-severe bun she always wore, her clothes excessively dowdy. Cardinal didn't know exactly how old she was, but she was certainly on the shelf, which suited him just fine. He didn't need his wife getting jealous, or Myrtle deciding to leave and have babies.

"Yes?" Cardinal asked her.

"Mr. McDougall is here to see you." She looked worried and apologetic. "Should I tell him—"

McDougall had apparently decided not to wait for her to announce him. He pushed past her into the room with a pile of documents held in one hand.

"Sir," Myrtle said, a bit desperately. "Sir, Mr. Cardinal is—"

"It's fine, Myrtle." Cardinal put down his pipe and stood. "Close the door."

She scurried out with a worried look and shut the door behind her.

"What is it now?" Cardinal asked from between gritted teeth. It had already been a terrible day, so why did he have to endure a visit from McDougall on top of everything else?

McDougall slapped the pile of documents down on the desk. "You need to shut down construction. *Immediately*!"

"After all these years." Cardinal groaned. "I can't believe you came all the way—"

McDougall flipped to a design page, heedless of Cardinal's protestations. "There are increasing distortions in all key structural members on the bridge. Here, here, and here."

Despite himself, Cardinal leaned forward to look. His brows snapped together.

"This can't be right." He shook his head. "No, no—these beams must already have been bent before they were installed."

"I oversaw the manufacturing of them *personally*," McDougall gritted out. "They were installed prior to your departure. I've been contacted by a man at Kahnawake. Something is wrong."

There was a moment of fear before Cardinal scoffed at him. "I have a man on the job."

"Alec Durand," McDougall said bitterly. "A green novice who should never have been handed a project so complex, and even he knew that the numbers didn't align."

Cardinal ignored that. "He would have told me if there was any such pressing issue as…"

He broke off, turning away in disbelief; his eyes landing at the envelopes stacked on the desk, and cold dread settled into the pit of his stomach when he noticed the name—

It was hardly ten minutes later that the two of them pushed their way through the door of the post office in haste, sending a woman reeling back with an angry cry.

McDougall waved his hands at her, muttering a brief apology, before catching up with Cardinal -who hadn't even noticed.

"Haven't you Canucks ever heard of a telegram?" Cardinal snarled at McDougall as they hurried for the desk. "Why would he send this in a damned letter?"

"Something for you to consider later," McDougall shot back, "if you ever work again!"

Cardinal wanted to spit insults at him, but there wasn't time, they were at the desk now. Through the window, he could see a clerk sorting mail.

"Young man!" Cardinal called.

The man gave a distracted nod to acknowledge them and held up a hand for them to wait.

"Turn around this instant!" Cardinal slapped the counter with the flat of his palm. At the worker's wide-eyed, insulted stare, he felt the need to yell in fury. "I have a matter of extreme urgency." He reached into his pocket and fumbled with his wallet. He could barely hold it, and McDougall had to take the paper from him and put it on the counter. "I need you to send a telegram to Quebec City. Immediately, do you understand?"

The worker stared at him, and it was McDougall who broke the silence.

"Now, goddammit," he snapped. "It's a matter of life and death!"

Mary Young yawned and leaned against the desk. Her shifts had been too long since Edith had gone off and gotten married, and the postmaster told her that there were no replacements applying for the job.

The bell rang at the Baudot keyboard in the corner of the room and then it suddenly lurched into movement. Mary wandered over to it and shut off the bell, leaning on the desk as the words printed onto the telegram card.

When it stopped, she plucked the card out of the machine and stared at it. Her eyes traveled over the message once, then another time, and her face went pale.

"Clarence!" Her voice rose in a hysterical yell. "Clarence, where are you?"

"Ma'am?" The telegram boy looked over from where he'd been dozing.

"The bridge." Mary's hands were shaking so hard she could barely hold the telegram. "You need to take this to the bridge. Now. *Now*!" She ran across the room and pulled him off his seat. "*Now*," she repeated.

"Mary," one of the men said. "What is—"

"Now!" Mary yelled at Clarence. She shooed him out of the room, running at his heels, and burst out into the sunshine with him. When he went for his bike, she shook her head and grabbed for his arm, pointing to a black and white horse who was standing lazily in the sun. "No, take Domino!"

The men came out the door behind them and one of them boosted Clarence into the saddle before smacking a hand on the horse's withers to send it galloping away with Clarence clutching the pommel.

"Mary, what is it?" The man looked back at her.

"The bridge," Mary whispered. She shook her head. "It's the bridge."

○

On the street, Ginette heard the screams of annoyance and looked up just in time to see the telegram boy thunder past on the black-and-white horse.

"Horsey!" Luc said excitedly. "Where's the horsey going, Mama?"

"He's going…" Ginette looked down the street. The telegram boy leaned into a turn and people scattered out of the way. The bridge lay down that road, and…what else?

No. It was only the bridge.

She swallowed hard. "I don't know, sweetheart," she lied, and her arm tightened around Etienne as cold fear grew in her chest.

○

At the bridge, a huge team was accompanying a section of the bridge as it was moved into place to be lifted. Horses strained and men hooked the carrying cables around hydraulic jacks. This was as much an art as a science, hard-won lessons in safety mixing with an intuition of which cable might be a bit weak, which specific place on the beam might be best for the cable. The men shouted to one another without looking up, the language of the jobsite and their familiarity with one another helping them move as one unit.

On a hill overlooking both the river and the site, Alec stood with his hands in the pockets of his suit pants. His eyes were fixed on the bridge, and there was a frown on his face. He shifted slowly but continuously: crossing his arms, then putting his hands back in his pockets, shifting his weight.

His eyes went back to Jean, time and again, and it wasn't long before the other man noticed him. Jean gave a reassuring nod in Alec's direction.

That made Alec feel worse. His chest had been a knot of anxiety all day, the tangle of thoughts layering over one another. Should he have started back up? Should he, indeed, have started back up weeks ago? Would the board dismiss him without references for holding up the process? He should have made his decision earlier and he still wasn't sure of it. Eventually, he wandered away in a slow circle, watching his shoes, lost in thought.

The clop of a horse's hooves sounded and a whistle split the air.

Alec looked up to see a young telegram boy on horseback, both horse and rider sweaty from the ride.

He cleared his throat; between the dust and the heat, it was dry. "Can I help you?"

The boy held up an envelope. "I have a telegram for the site engineer. Ms. Mary said to come as quick as I could."

"That's me." Alec strode over to take the telegram, and, as he tore it open, looked over to where the beam was now being lifted.

The groan began so slowly that it seemed to come from inside the bones of those present. Men began to turn to look before they knew what they were looking at and Alec, scanning the telegram, lifted his head like a deer listening for footsteps. The horse pranced nervously and the boy reined it in sharply.

There was a pause while the world seemed to hang in complete stillness…and then the groan rose to a metallic screech, accompanied by the indrawn, horrified breath of every man on site. Alec burst into motion, the telegram dropping from his fingers, and sprinted for the slope, but even as he was moving, so was the bridge: sliding, twisting, toppling.

Yells of alarm came from the crews on the bridge, and the moment seemed at once frozen in time and over in an eyeblink. The structure collapsed in on itself, solid metal warping and twisting out of shape with terrifying force as workers flung themselves clear of the collapse.

Alec could hear all of it and none of it. He was only dimly aware of his feet striking the ground. There were shadows bobbing in the water and screams for help, pieces of debris casting shadows for a split second and obliterating those beneath without ceremony or mercy. The crew on the shore was running for the water, but they were too slow, all of them were too slow.

From the top of the bridge, there came a yell and Alec's gaze was drawn up.

Jean.

The section of bridge buckled and Jean's arms windmilled. There was an indrawn breath from around Alec, and a gasp as Jean toppled, only to grab onto one of the beams. He hung, the beam creaking and bending.

"JEAN!" Alec bellowed.

The other workers were reaching out for him, holding up their hands to catch him, but he would never survive the fall. Alec leapt for the beams and began to climb. The structure was tipping and there was no safety behind him, no safety ahead of him.

There was a groan that made every hair on his arms stand up, and the structure gave a sickening lurch. Alec had grabbed onto one of the bars, bracing himself for a fall, and his eyes were still squeezed shut when he heard screams from the shore. He saw them pointing and was able to track two figures on their way into the water: one flailing, trying to catch hold of anything to save himself, the other already limp.

The bridge gave another twist and Alec was jolted back into motion. Jean. He needed to get to Jean, who was still clinging to the steel bar. He had seen the others fall, and now he watched Alec approaching as if it were a mirage.

"Jean!" Alec called. He grabbed a pylon and leaned out as far as he could. "Take my hand!"

"Alec!" Jean swung towards him, and his arms clenched as the beam creaked again.

His hand locked onto Alec's and not a moment too soon, for the beam twisted downward alarmingly and Jean swung out into empty air. With his entire weight on Alec's hand, Alec stumbled and fell. His hand clenched around Jean's wrist and Jean's shout of agony was matched only by Alec's as he fell, face-first, onto another beam.

The two men looked at one another, their eyes locked, the breath hot in their lungs.

"Alec," Jean called again. His voice was barely audible. "I'm scared."

Blindsided by the memory of their first day working together, Alec smiled. I'm scared, he had said to Jean, and Jean had said…what? There were tears in his eyes. "That's good," he told Jean. "It's good to be scared of the drop. You told me that, remember?"

Jean laughed as well, but there was a sob in it. "I don't want to die—"

His words cut off as the beam shuddered and dropped a foot, and the crowd on the shore gave a scream.

Alec made a split-second decision. "Our only chance is the water!"

"What?" Jean yelled. His feet kicked against empty air.

"It's going to buckle," Alec called. "We don't have time to climb down. I'll swing you out!"

Jean's eyes were wide with panic, but he nodded, and Alec gritted his teeth and yelled in pain as he put all of the force in his body behind the swing of his arm.

"One—two—*three*!"

He let go of Jean's hand and Jean tumbled toward the water. It took a moment of falling for Alec to realize that he was following in Jean's wake—that the sound in his ears was the unholy shriek of metal bending and twisting and shearing and tearing. The water rushed up to meet him and he put out his hands uselessly.

J ean plunged into muddy water. He opened his
eyes, only to see something rushing toward him.
He flinched, but nothing hit him. Had it been a
shadow? Had the swirl of water carried it away
from—

A girder hit him across the back and his mouth
opened in a yell of pain, only for precious air to
escape his mouth, and his lungs to begin drawing in
the water around him. He coughed and flailed, and
somehow came up above the water, buoyed by the air
in his clothing or the force of the currents, but
certainly not his own machinations.

"Alec!" The word came out as a croak, he was
choking on water. He flailed, looking around himself.
"Alec!" Pieces of the bridge were raining down
around them, small and large alike. Screams sounded
from the shore, and he thought he heard his name.
"*ALEC!*"

Nothing.

Jean managed to take a breath before diving back
into the water. He looked around, this time making
out dim shapes; he was close enough to the surface
that the light still penetrated through the silt the
collapse had thrown up.

There! A shirt, billowing in the water. Jean swam
down, already fighting the pressure in his lungs. He
could see dark hair, the glint of a gold ring. Alec was
pinned under one of the girders, and terribly still, but
Jean grabbed the girder and yanked. It didn't move,
the end having sunk into the silt, and he tried again—

His lungs were on fire.

He grabbed for Alec's hand now, and yanked at it desperately, but Alec did not move. His lips were open, no air coming from them. Jean pulled with all his might, only for the ring to come off in his hand.

If he stayed here, he was going to die. With a last, agonized look, he pushed off the riverbed and emerged into the air with a wheezing gasp. There was yelling all around him and he stumbled out of the river like a drunkard before dropping to his knees on the ground.

"Alec!"

It was a woman's voice he heard, and he frowned. Was he hallucinating? The whole world was vibrating.

"Alec!" A woman dropped to her knees in front of him. Her hair curled around her face. She was tiny, delicate, holding a baby to her chest. "Where is Alec? They said he saved you."

Jean stared at her in mute horror. Beyond his volition, his hand came up and unclenched to show the ring in his palm, twisted and bent.

The woman gave a scream. She sank down into the mud, fingers around the back of the baby's head, weeping and weeping as the men pulled her and her sons away from the remnants of the construction.

CHAPTER 28

Ben shoved himself back from the table. His heart was racing and he thought he was going to be sick. He pressed the back of his hand over his mouth and gulped for air. Oddly, it was Esther's voice that steadied him. She wasn't here, but he could almost hear her: *Ben, you can't throw up on the reference materials. They're priceless. They've been so carefully stored.*

It was enough distraction for him to steady his stomach. He pressed a hand over it and sat up. Jean, Alec, Ginette… But what about Theodore Cardinal? He scrabbled through the reference materials, looking for anything, anything.

A letter was there, something from his great grandmother, and he settled down to read it.

Theodore Cardinal hunched over his cigarette and tried to light it. The tremble in his hands never left him now. He had given up on packing a pipe and used cigarettes instead. He did not look around himself at the room. He had decorated it years ago to fit a career he no longer savored. Everything he had built surrounded him like a too-small prison instead of the castle he had intended.

A sound made him turn. Lillian stood there, her dress as proper as it always was, her bearing regal. Where Theodore had gone bald and hunched with age far before his time, she was still young. No young girl from the schoolroom, of course, but a mother who wore her new role with quiet dignity.

A heavy envelope was in her hands.

"Hello, darling." The sight of her was one of the few things that still made him smile, though the envelope set off the too-familiar flutter in his chest.

"The Royal Commission of Inquiry has completed their investigation." She held up the envelope and waited for his nod before taking out the report and handing it to him.

His eyes scanned the pages. He cared nothing for the mountain of words, all prettily arranged, until he got to the last pages:

a)   Design of the chords that failed were made by S. Glover, the designing engineer of the Phoenix Bridge Company.

b)   Design was examined and officially approved by Mr. Theodore Cardinal, consulting engineer of the Quebec Bridge and Railway Company.

c)   Failure cannot be attributed directly to any cause other than errors in judgement on the part of these two engineers.

His heart squeezed and Cardinal dropped the papers onto the desk before him. There, in plain words, was the truth, the very thing he had run from, the thing he had prayed would never become public knowledge. They knew it, of course, everyone knew it, but while the commission investigated, there was still hope—

"There's no penal sanction." Lillian's voice was like cool water, but uncertainty touched it for the first time. "I thought you would be relieved."

He looked up at her and felt the urge to apologize for everything, for the fact that he had chained her to a failure, a man old before his time, instead of giving her the life they had both dreamed of. He shook his head, both at that thought, and at her words: "There will be no relief in this, I fear."

Lillian did not flinch. She leaned down to kiss his head and he smelled the scent of her, the powder-and-rose of her soap, the sun-dried silk of her gown. She knew better than to journey with him into the darkness of this conversation again, and so she merely said,

"They're ready in the family room, whenever you are."

He sat alone when she had gone, and then left without looking at the report on the desk. He could feel the darkness threatening to swamp him again. He had seen nothing of the collapse, but he had imagined every moment, and if he stopped to reflect now…

He would go mad.

In the family room, Lillian sat with their son on her lap, bouncing him. It was a study in contrasts, her posture and manners honed by years with private governesses and tutors, and her simple happiness as she beheld her son. Near the window, a photographer waited with his camera box and a flash lamp.

Cardinal took a deep breath before joining Lillian at the chair. He laid his hand on it and looked down at his son, a boy staring up at him with Lillian's almond-shaped eyes. That gave him the courage he needed to speak.

"I have been thinking."

"Yes?" She looked up at him, still smiling from looking at Geoffrey. Her smile faded. "Teddy, what is it?"

"Perhaps he should take your name," Cardinal told her.

She swallowed, but whatever she was planning to say was cut off by the photographer.

"Ready?"

She turned back, her chin rising and her socialite smile on her face, holding Geoffrey proudly as the photographer bent to look into the view.

"On three," he told them, his voice muffled. "One, two—"

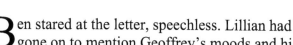

B en stared at the letter, speechless. Lillian had gone on to mention Geoffrey's moods and his sleep, as well as other family matters, but that had been the end of it. A name change, a mask against the legacy, and Cardinal had faced nothing more. He'd lived in luxury for the rest of his life while Alec was dead.

He did not want to read any more, but the documents called to him. Alec's journal had looked like nothing to him. What if there were more answers here?

CHAPTER 29

December 3, 1919

The crowd that huddled at one side of the bridge was all bundled in formal winter wear, insufficient against the chill of the December day. A reporter bent over his photography equipment and breathed on his hands to warm them before taking a picture of the crowd. It was a pity the image would not capture the crisp blue of the sky, but the iron struts still stood out well.

A red ribbon stretched across one of the two railway tracks, tied with an ornate bow, and a single engine puffed steam as it waited for the ribbon to be cut.

On the stage, several men stood in clothes that were even more formal: Canadian government officials, an engineer, and a man with cleanly-coiffed blond hair and heavy-lidded blue eyes, his bearing military-straight. The Prince of Wales might be away from the battle front, but he was showing this event the respect it deserved. After all, the supplies ferried across this bridge would be vital to the war effort, and there was already an armed guard posted at either side to make sure that no sabotage could be carried out.

Archibald McDougall finished speaking quietly with the Canadian officials and, at the Prince of Wales' nod, approached the podium to address the crowd.

He could see the others shivering, but he did not feel the cold. He could not feel much at all, in fact. His mind was not on the structure behind him, but on the one that had once been there, lines distorted and struts placed ever so slightly differently. His mind was not on this chilly day, but instead, in the still heat of summer, the sort of day when the failed bridge had come tumbling down.

He had not been there, had not seen that event, but he dreamed of it nearly every night. He did not need to see it. He had spent so much time sketching out the bent struts that he could picture exactly how it had collapsed.

What his mind could not have imagined was Alec Durand's climb. McDougall could remember the man, tall and strapping, slamming a sledgehammer down with single-minded focus. He remembered Alec's early reports, the smudges that showed oft-erased numbers.

It seemed beyond belief that Alec had climbed the twisting struts to save one of the workers, and had been lost with dozens of others in the muddy water, crushed by the remnants of the bridge. Nothing would bring those men back to their widows and their children.

McDougall had come back here to take over construction, to run this project differently. He would not allow any of the same mistakes to occur. He had made sure to stand between the labourers and the city officials who wanted to cut costs.

It was all he could do for the memory of the lost. He wrapped his fingers around the edge of the podium and gazed out at the crowd. They might never understand what this project meant, but he would.

"Ladies and gentlemen," he began, "it's been more than 10 years since the Canadian government took over construction of this bridge and bestowed the responsibility of completing it on me. A great deal of my life has gone into this project, which feels quite like a Phoenix rising from the ashes."

He looked out over the crowd and noticed some signs waving in the back. He was sure he had not seen those a few moments ago and he felt a prickle of disquiet. Were these anti-monarchy picketers, malcontents who resented the Empire drawing Canada into European affairs? Such a disturbance would be an embarrassment.

He looked over to where the security guards were standing and saw that they had noticed the picketers as well. That was good. They would take care of any incidents. After all, they had accompanied the prince to more hostile places than this.

McDougall cleared his throat and bent back to speak into the microphone. "And now, it is with great honour that I invite His Royal Highness, the Prince of Wales, to step forward and officially open the Quebec Bridge."

Edward stepped forward and McDougall handed the scissors to him respectfully. He watched as the prince went to the red ribbon and cut it so that it fluttered down in the crisp air. Cheers and applause

sounded from the crowd and the waiting rail engine
began to move. It crept forward at first as it gained
power, and then steamed down the rail line, across the
bridge.

McDougall's heart had been in his throat while he
watched the bridge take its weight, but each
measurement here had been double- and triple-
checked by multiple engineers. This bridge was
sound. The curse that had afflicted the bridge was
lifted, at long last.

He was still clapping when there was a commotion
and the picketers burst through the front line of the
crowd, with a very unexpected vanguard: a small,
delicate woman whose pale skin nearly glowed
against the black clothes she was wearing.

Security moved toward her, and McDougall held
up a hand to hold them back before he realized what
he was doing.

This woman. He knew this woman.

Ginette Durand ripped at a chain around her neck
and it broke. She threw it at McDougall's feet and the
pendant on the necklace clinked as it struck the
podium. McDougall bent to pick it up, not realizing at
first what it was, and then trembling when he saw
what he held in his hand: a battered, crumpled
wedding ring.

He shook. It had been 12 years. There could not
possibly be blood on this ring any longer, but he
swore he could see it glinting in the scratches and
dents. He closed his hand around it, though he wanted
to throw the thing away from him, and met Ginette's
angry eyes.

"This bridge is stained with the blood of the men who died for it!" Ginette called. She turned, appealing to the crowd, and threw a hand out to point at the podium. "They won't even name those who sacrificed their lives in the name of progress—the men like my husband, Alec Durand!"

McDougall swallowed hard.

Ginette turned to him. "I know you saw the flaws, Mr. McDougall. And how much more blood must be spilled for these projects? How many more wives must be widowed in the name of glory? How many sons will grow without knowing their fathers?"

The crowd parted behind her, and a weathered man limped forward. At his right walked a young boy with long limbs, already tall, and with the coltish look of one who had not yet finished growing, while a slightly younger boy held onto the man's hand.

McDougall had never seen these two boys, but he knew of them. Their names had been in Alec's obituary: *is survived by his wife, Ginette, his sons, Luc and Etienne, his father...*

He closed his eyes, hoping this was like the nightmares that plagued him, but Ginette was still there when he opened them again. What was in her eyes was not rage, which would have been easier to bear, but instead, a call through the years. She knew, he realized, with a start. She was the one who had seen him argue with Theodore Cardinal in the café all those years ago.

And she wanted him to give voice to the truth, in the memory of those lost.

"How many, Mr. McDougall?" she asked him again, softly. She turned on her heel and left, the boys trailing in her wake, as the picketers picked up a chant. It took only moments for the crowd to disperse; no one wanted to be a part of this. The smell of the engine still lingered in the air, but the joy of the opening was entirely gone.

Evening found him alone in his office, where he took the misshapen ring out of his pocket. There were no real drops of blood on its surface. It was only a ring, cleaned well, worn bright by fingers rubbing over its surface; he pictured Ginette, alone at a table, holding it in her palm when the boys had gone to bed.

Twelve years, and she still grieved as deeply as he did.

No, he corrected himself, more deeply. She had lost her husband that day. Her sons might not even remember their father. Alec had been a kind man, he would have been a good father.

He walked over to his desk and set the ring on it. He had tidied everything today before going to the ceremony. He had almost approached the cleaning as its own ceremony: he filed each blueprint and report—his secretary did not ever touch those—in the correct place and knew the project to be over.

Now this.

He tried to sit, but could not settle. What was he here to do? He could not simply wait—inaction would drive him mad. Nor was there anything to do about the loss of Alec's life. It was done, the funerals completed, the widows given a pittance as compensation, and McDougall had believed somehow that the successful completion of the bridge would put their ghosts to rest. He saw, now, how wrong he had been.

There was a poem he had comforted himself with many times in the years since the disaster. In the first years after, it had not existed, and then a friend had sent it to him in a new book of poems, and McDougall had read it with the sense of dawn breaking on a dark night

"If—" the title read, and it wound through the trails and travails of a modern life. What was it to live, but to be surrounded by chaos, by hate and doubt, by traps? What was it to be human, but to be caught up in the petty squabbles of others?

"Or walk with Kings," McDougall murmured, "nor lose the common touch." Had he not stood, today, with the Prince of Wales and thought himself very important? He had believed that the attention of the crown showed the success of his work, and he had forgotten the blood that once swirled in the waters of the river.

He went to the bookshelf and took out the book. It was beginning to be tattered at the edges. He was, by nature, fastidiously neat, but he had read it many times. The book even fell open to the poem. Now he did sit, to read it once more, and he mouthed the words into the empty room and the silence of the building.

When he was finished, he sat back in his chair and contemplated the night sky outside the windows. He had been given the gift of solitude tonight, to contemplate the fact that the job was not finished.

He reached out to pick up the ring again and held it in his palm. An idea was taking shape in his head. He had completed only one project, and he had maintained, through his own discipline, the communication that would prevent another disaster.

But other project managers did not have the same caution. They did not carry as heavy a burden, and they might think of the disaster as nothing to do with them, a sign of a backwards province. He did not intend to allow them to keep their ignorance. Instead, he would bring the memory of those lost lives forward forever.

He pulled a piece of paper toward him, uncapped his pen, and began the letter:

Dear Mr. Kipling—

Weeks later, he looked around his office and straightened one stack of paper at the edge of his desk. Everything was neat—excessively so, in fact. He could not focus on anything except the meeting ahead of him.

There was a murmur of voices from outside the door and his heart began to speed. It was time. He stood as his secretary opened the door.

"Mrs. Durand here to see you, sir."

"Thank you, Clara." He nodded at her and linked his hands behind his back.

Clara stood aside to let Ginette past her, and then left the two of them in the quiet of the study.

"Thank you for coming to meet with me," McDougall said. Words seemed monumentally inadequate right now.

Ginette lifted her chin slightly. She was small, perhaps slightly softened at the edges by the passing of the years, but still delicately made. She was wearing black again, and McDougall wondered if she had never put off mourning after Alec died.

"Would you like refreshments?" McDougall gestured to the table. "There's tea."

Ginette hesitated, then shook her head.

"Please, sit." He crossed to the little cluster of couches around the table, and chose a seat, himself.

When she came to join him, her movements were graceful and self-assured. She folded her hands in her lap and looked at him gravely. "I was surprised by your letter," she told him. "I had not expected an apology from anyone involved in my husband's death."

McDougall sighed and looked down at the rug for a moment before meeting her eyes once more. "Mrs. Durand, your...demonstration...showed me how misguided my efforts had been to atone for the deaths of the workers on the bridge. I had told myself that, by completing the project with more stringent standards, I could make things right."

She said nothing, but her jaw had clenched.

"But those who died..." McDougall said softly. "They died for someone else's dream. The dream was Theodore Cardinal's. It was mine. It was the dream of the Phoenix Bridge Company. Building the bridge did nothing to set those souls to rest."

"There is no rest for them," Ginette told him, and her voice broke on the words. "There has been no justice, and nothing will bring them back."

"I see that now. What I also see, that you do not, is how many other lives have been—could be—lost every day, on every project. That is not to call you

ignorant, Mrs. Durand. It is simply that I have been a
fixture on many job sites, and I have seen the ways
the squabbles between management have put the
workers at risk."

Her eyes had narrowed.

"You asked me how many more wives would be
widowed," he told her bluntly, "and how many more
sons would not know their fathers, and it was a good
question, one to which I did not have an answer. I
cannot atone for your husband's death, Mrs.
Durand—there is no atonement for that—but I can
work to ensure that the danger is ended, and that no
such disaster ever happens again."

"What do you propose?" Her hands were clasped
tightly in her lap.

"Are you familiar with the works of Rudyard
Kipling?"

She nodded once.

"Mr. Kipling has written about labourers and
engineers," McDougall explained. "The day you
confronted me, that very day, I wrote a letter to him. I
begged him to write a piece in commemoration of
those who toil so that others may live easily." He
picked up the sheet of paper from the desk and held it
out to her. "Please."

She pursed her lips slightly and read.

"A vow for yourself?" she asked at last.

McDougall shook his head.

"And…Esdras." She pointed at the biblical
citation. "What is the verse? I am not familiar with
it."

He reached for the bible and handed it to her.
There was a marker at the passage, and she read in

silence, though her lips moved. He waited until he heard the book close and then he looked back at her. She was sitting with her back ramrod straight. Wind whistled slightly outside the window and sleet pattered on the glass; spring was coming slowly. She looked out at the sky and closed her eyes, lashes breaking like a wave over one pale cheek. There were tears in her lashes.

"I cannot help but think what Alec would have said of that passage," she said, without opening her eyes. "For if ever a man could have weighed fire, it would be him. He had a rare gift, Mr. McDougall, and it shone in him too briefly."

"And there is naught I can do to bring him back," McDougall told her. "I've no doubt you would trade my life for his, could it be done—"

"And doom another woman to mourn? Other children?" She did not meet his eyes. "You think very little of me, Mr. McDougall."

He was shamed by that. "Very well. There were times when I would have made the trade, if I could—but I cannot. What I can do is remind my fellow engineers of the burden they *must* bear and the honour they *must* hold, if they are to perform this work. It is what should have been expected of myself and of Theodore Cardinal." He cleared his throat slightly. "He was unable to…be here today."

"He does not want to face those he wronged." Her tone was bitter. "Well, whatever else I could say of you, Mr. McDougall, at least you were willing to listen to my words."

"And to act on them." He nodded to her. "This oath—this ceremony—was written for all new engineers within the commonwealth."

Her eyes searched his. "This…"

McDougall went to the desk and picked up a box. His hands were shaking slightly while he carried it back to her. He handed it over: plain, but well-made, held closed by a brass clasp. She set down the paper and took the box, only to draw in a shuddering breath at the sight of a ring inside.

Alec Durand's wedding band lay on a bed of black velvet—except, it was not the same ring Ginette once carried around her neck. The dented and scratched gold piece that Ginette had found difficult to look at without imagining the violence of Alec's death. The pure metal had since been melted down and reformed into a new shape that now appeared unified and strong. A pattern across the ring resembled the arches of an aqueduct, a structure that had supported human life throughout history. Ginette reached inside the box and picked it up curiously.

"We call it, 'The Iron Ring'," McDougall told her, "to be worn on the littlest finger of an engineer's drafting hand. Built roughly, designed to catch." He watched her turn it over in her hands, feeling the rough ridges. "A constant reminder to take care in one's work."

Ginette looked up at him. "Every engineering student in the commonwealth," she said finally. "That is your goal, Mr. McDougall? To have every engineer remember the tragedy that took those lives? To carry the reminder of it with them, as constant as grief?"

"So that no more widows may grieve," McDougall told her. "Or sons. Your children…"

She closed her eyes for a moment and he could see how close the grief was to her, always. "They tell me they miss their father, but they never had the chance to know him. Luo remembers little. Etienne…all he could possibly remember is being held, or being sung to. Alec would sing to him, though his voice was never…" Her voice broke on the words, and she put the gold ring down in the box.

McDougall sat once more. "You have not remarried."

She heard the question. "It felt an insult to Alec—and then…then, I was so filled with anger over the bridge, that I knew I could not give my heart to anyone else."

"Will you be free of it now?" He was hopeful.

When she met his gaze again, her expression was one of cool amusement, and she did not answer the question. She stood. "I thank you for this meeting. This…is a fitting tribute to my husband."

"I would like it if you could be there, for our first ceremony in Montreal." He stood as well. "And your sons. The Ritual of the Calling of an Engineer."

She hesitated only for a moment before nodding. "Very well. I should like to see those who will someday hold others' lives in their hands." She offered the box with Alec's ring back to McDougall, who shook his head.

"The ring is yours," McDougall told her. "It is the first and only of its kind, as the rest shall be made from iron." He paused for a moment. "It should have been his."

Ginette said nothing, only took the box with her and left the office with quick, quiet steps, and McDougall went back to his desk to stare out at the gloomy day.

Come May, in fairer weather, a new class of engineers would take this oath under the watchful eye of Ginette Durand. How many would know her name, and what she represented? Perhaps none—in name. But, long after the memory of Alec had faded, the engineers of the commonwealth would carry his legacy on.

○

In the darkness of the library's lower level, Ben sat back in his chair and rubbed at his face. He did not know how long it had been since he began reading; away from the daylight, or the regular buzzing of his phone, he had no way to gauge the passage of time.

Alec had died. The beautiful marriage Ben had witnessed so briefly between Alec and Ginette had been snuffed out on a hot, August day, and what remained was a ceremony and a dented ring.

He returned the materials in silence and took the stairs up to the main floor very slowly.

This, then, was the cost of ambition without responsibility. This was what his father had so often derided after a drink or two as "the complaining of people who cannot create." It was, horrifyingly, what Ben had wanted for years: to be someone of Cardinal's stature, unquestioned, able to send out blueprints and relax in an elegant study while others dealt with paperwork and regulations.

He swallowed and squeezed his eyes shut for a moment, then shook his head to clear it.

He wasn't going to be that man. He had proven that He had taken the first step away from those ghosts today, and he had been granted a chance to continue down this new path.

He was going to make the most of it.

CHAPTER 30

"Ready?" Steve asked. His camera was held up to his eye and he was leaning back into the crush of families while Ben and his mother posed for a shot.

"One moment." Tracey pulled away from Ben and turned his head with both hands. She smoothed his hair down and then, to his utter mortification, licked her thumb and rubbed something off his cheek.

"Mom!" he protested.

"Oh, don't you give me that." She put her arm around his waist. "What are mothers for, if not embarrassing their children?"

"You could try not embarrassing me," Ben muttered, but his mouth was twitching. How many times had he been through this? Junior high graduation, high school, birthdays, dances... His mother had been there to make each one of them special, even when Ben saw no point, even when he thought it was ridiculous.

And now, instead of the sea of forgettable days and enduring bitterness, the feeling that his parents should be together, that they would be if Tracy had just understood Ben's father, that Ben's father wouldn't have left if she had just been more accepting…

Now, he had the memories of the birthday cakes and parties, he had the pictures of him every year, he had so much more than he would have if she hadn't been there.

He squeezed her in a one-armed hug. "You know you're not really embarrassing me, right?"

She kissed his cheek, and something in her expression said that she knew the general drift of his thoughts. Then she pointed to where Steve was still waiting. "Okay, smile."

Ben plastered on a smile and blinked when the flash went off. It always confused him that Steve, a technophile if ever there was one, used an actual camera instead of his phone.

"Stay there," Steve called, "I'm going to take a couple more."

He took enough more that Ben was seeing spots by the time it was over. He was glad he had already gotten his diploma, since it would have been difficult to walk across the stage when he couldn't see properly. Hopefully, he would be able to complete the Iron Ring ceremony without any incidents.

He looked down at the diploma in his hands. It almost didn't seem real that everything was over. Senior week had been a blur of road trips, pub crawls, and sleeping late, with the midday diversion of packing up and cleaning his apartment whilst wildly hungover.

If he never smelled Lysol again, it would be too soon.

"Hey, guys." Tyler appeared, dressed in a ripped band t-shirt and jeans. Apparently, he had decided to be as ostentatiously out-of-uniform as possible.

"Tyler." Ben's mouth went dry. "I didn't…see you today. Hi."

"Hey." Tyler shrugged, his hands in his pockets. "I liked this place so much, I decided to do a victory lap next year."

Ben stared at him for a moment until he realized what was going on. "Oh, God. Are you—did you—"

"Flunked the midterms." Tyler shrugged, though he had the affect of someone who was working hard not to be bothered. "Hard to come back from that. Anyway." He looked over Ben's shoulder. "Mrs. O'Betany—I mean, Mrs. Harris—hi."

"Tyler!" Ben's mother went to give him a hug. "It's so good to see you."

Tyler endured the hug with good grace. "So— proud of your graduate, eh?"

"Very." She looked over at Ben with her face shining, and then visibly remembered Tyler's graduation status. "So…what are *your* plans for the summer?"

Ben winced, but Tyler only gave a wave of his hand. "Boring and depressing. Get a cheap apartment somewhere, see about getting a part-time job, get the remedial classes all set up…apparently, purgatory is just a slow grind. I'll be hanging out with Ben, though, if he ends up sticking around in the city for a while."

Ben crossed his fingers. He'd had two interviews in the past week, with one more lined up next week.

One was with a firm in Quebec, while the others were in New York and Chicago.

"I can't tell if he's crossing his fingers that he gets to stay and hang out with me," Tyler said in a stage whisper, "or that he gets to run away."

Ben gave him a look.

"Anyway, how about I get a group shot, huh?" Tyler reached for Steve's camera.

"I'd love that," Tracey said enthusiastically.

Steve set about demonstrating the camera's various capabilities to Tyler, who looked flummoxed by the old-school technology. Ben and Tracey watched in amusement, until Tyler nodded and took the camera. He held it in one hand and ushered them all into position with the grandiose gestures of an orchestra conductor.

After the last photograph, his eyes focused over Ben's shoulder and his face got wary. Turning, Ben saw Esther. She was taking pictures with her family. Her sister was presently trying to get her to do some dance routine for a video, and Esther was shaking her head emphatically.

He froze when Esther looked up, as if sensing his gaze on her. The two of them stared at one another for a moment before Esther gave a half-smile and nodded, and Ben nodded back.

"She seems nice," his mother said finally, making Ben jump. He had forgotten the rest of them were there. "What's her name?"

Ben looked at Tyler. "I don't suppose I could get some help, here."

"Nope." Tyler shook his head. "Nope. Nope, nope, nope."

"Thanks, man, it's always nice to know I have the support of my best friend."

Tyler gave an obsequious bow and came to give the camera back to Steve before disappearing into the crowd with a wave.

"Do you not want to talk about this, sweetie?" Ben's mother asked a moment later. Given the fact that Ben's face had flushed bright red, it wasn't difficult for her to see that something was amiss.

"I, uh…it's fine. It's not anything, though."

"Maybe you should go talk to her," his mother suggested. "Introduce yourself to her family. Her parents might like that."

"I don't think so." Ben gave her a one-armed hug. "Nothing is *going* to happen with her."

"Ben." His mother took him by the shoulders. "I try not to give you too much overbearing life advice. I don't want to be one of those parents. But…I think you should go meet her parents and talk to her."

Ben shook his head. "Nope."

"Ben, sweetie, she's the valedictorian, isn't she? So, she's smart, and she's very pretty…." She looked over at her husband. "Help me out."

"Oh, no. No." Steve shook his head. "No, I don't think that's wise."

Ben gave him a grateful nod. "See? Steve gets it."

Ben's mother did not look exceedingly pleased with their agreement. "Mmm. Well, all I'm saying is, don't let her be the one that got away."

There was the sound of Esther's laughter and Ben looked over to where she was now doing the dance with her sister. The two of them did a complicated piece of footwork and a spin. Yasmine was clearly the performer of the two of them, with Esther looking unsure of herself, but her fondness for her sister was clear. Their father held the phone to record, and their mother was clapping a beat and calling out encouragement to the two of them.

There was an ache in Ben's chest, but this one wasn't as deep a wound as some he had been carrying. Watching Esther live a life entirely different from his wasn't precisely fun, but it didn't feel quite as wrong as he had expected.

"Sometimes the one who got away…" Ben shrugged. "…Is exactly the kick in the ass you need."

"Ben. Language!"

Ben rolled his eyes. "It's a perfectly reasonable expression, Mom. But, sorry. Anyway, that's how it is."

His mother looked over at Esther, uncertain now. "If you're sure, sweetie."

"I am." Surprisingly, it was true. He nodded to where the crowd was starting to move. "Ready for the ceremony?"

"Yes!" Steve's eyes lit up. "I did some reading on it, but it's kept very secret."

"Yep." Ben smiled. "I'll tell you about it while we walk, and…" He saw Tyler, lingering a little ways away. "One moment."

Tyler watched as Ben approached. "Hey."

"Hey." Ben grimaced. "It was good to see you." The two of them had spent the past week studiously avoiding one another.

"Isn't it?" Tyler said, spreading his arms as if to bask in adoration. He chuckled at himself, and sobered. "I…yeah, it's good to see you, too. And it wasn't all that awkward. Not as awkward as your mom ribbing you about Esther. Never landed that plane, did you?"

"Tyler…"

"Sorry, sorry."

"And I'm sorry," Ben said. He looked Tyler in the eyes. "I shouldn't have hit you."

"Eh." Tyler looked up at the sky, his eyes tracing a contrail. "Kind of surprised you didn't earlier. Maybe…" He looked back at Ben. "Maybe it's like the bridge, you know?"

"What?" Ben felt suddenly out of his depth.

"Sometimes you don't know there's a problem until some asshole screws everything up." Tyler scuffed at a clod of grass and sighed. "You're a good friend. I think I need to start paying attention to what matters, instead of—" He broke off and waved his hands, clearly at a loss for words.

"I know what you mean." Ben caught him up in a hug. "Love you, bro."

"Love you, too." Tyler's voice was muffled on Ben's graduation gown. "Idiot." He pulled away and both of them pretended they weren't blinking a suspicious sheen out of their eyes. "And…sorry about Esther. Seriously."

"Eh…." Ben shook his head.

"Whatever, man, chicks dig you. Even when you had that bowl cut in third grade." Tyler reached out to clap him on the shoulder. "You got this—but only if you don't miss the ceremony. Go on."

"Right. Thanks." Ben gave him a nod and jogged back to his mother and Steve. "Okay, where was I?

Right. The Iron Ring ceremony. So, turn of the 20th century, building a cantilevered bridge…"

CHAPTER 31

Liuna Station had the vaulted ceilings and ancient majesty of older buildings. Now converted into an event venue, it was still the site of the Iron Ring ceremony for Hamilton students every year, and Ben was impressed despite himself as he walked into the room where the ceremony would take place. This one had a lower ceiling, with pipes still visible and iron girders across the ceiling. There were chairs, set up neatly, and a dais, and an...

Anvil?

Ben looked at the anvil in surprise. It sat atop an altar, and metal chains had been attached to it. While the parents sat, the new graduates were ushered to stand in rows along the chains. Everyone waited in silence until the door opened to admit seven individuals—the seven wardens who would preside over the ritual. They sat at a long, elevated table behind the anvil, and the main warden held up a hammer for a moment.

When he lowered it, it was to tap out three letters on the table in morse code.

"S, S, T," said the warden. "It stands for steel, spirit, and time."

He held up the hammer to show that there was something chained to it: a single rivet, gone dark with age.

"This rivet comes from the bridge that triggered this tradition, called the Ritual of the Calling of an Engineer. The ritual is broken into three sections: the obligation, the charge, and the bestowing of the ring. We will begin with the oath. Graduates, please hold the chains in front of you."

The students reached out to take ahold of the chains.

"This chain symbolizes each engineer's obligation to help one another," the main warden told them.

Ben's eyes found Esther's in the crowd and they nodded to each other. They had not spoken since that day outside Professor McLeary's office, and that time had softened things between them, it seemed.

Tyler, he did not see at all. The other boy had hardly come out of his room during finals week, and Ben wondered now, guiltily, if Tyler would skip the ceremony on Ben's account.

"Repeat after me," the warden said, calling Ben's attention back to the ceremony. "I am an engineer. In my profession, I take deep pride. To it, I owe solemn obligations."

The graduates repeated the words.

"As an engineer, I pledge to practice integrity and fair dealing, tolerance and respect, and to uphold devotion to the standards and dignity of my profession."

Ben closed his eyes as he recited the words. The chorus of voices vibrated around him and rose to the rafters, and he could not help but feel purpose rising with it. Today, he was becoming one of a group, pledged to each other and to those their work served.

"I will always be conscious that my skill carries with it the obligation to serve humanity by making the best use of the Earth's precious wealth," Ben repeated after the warden. "As an engineer, I shall participate in none but honest enterprises. When needed, my skill and knowledge shall be given, without reservation, for the public good. In the performance of duty, and in fidelity to my profession, I shall give my utmost."

There was a silence when the oath concluded.

"We now invite the mentors." The warden stood. "Those of you who have been asked to present a ring, please come forward."

Ben felt a stab of envy as several members of the crowd stood. Despite himself, part of him still hoped that his father would stand up from the back of the room and come to stand among the mentors. He was not there, however, no matter how Ben's gaze searched the group of mentors and the corners of the room.

He looked down and told himself not to let his father's absence mar the day.

When Esther's was called, she radiated contentment as she walked across the stage. Ben had never seen her at peace before, and it was a strange transformation. Today, Esther was not striving to be anything—she simply was. When she took the ring, she looked out into the crowd and Ben saw a girl who must be her sister wave to her. Her mother was crying and smiling at the same time.

He watched the others go up, and when it was his turn, he let go of the chain and walked up to Professor McLeary.

"Congratulations," McLeary told him as he placed the ring in Ben's hand. "You produced an excellent essay on the role of ethics in engineering, Mr. O'Betany. I have great faith in you, and it is my pleasure to bestow this ring."

"Thank you, sir." Ben closed his fingers around the ring. "I learned a lot."

As he went to the side of the stage, he looked out one more time. This time, however, he did not search for his father. He looked, instead, at his mother and Steve, who waved back at him, and Ben smiled. His father was not here, but they were. They were, and Professor McLeary was, with kind words for Ben.

It seemed only moments later that he was out in the sunlight, blinking as the students and their families mingled. Refreshment tables served lemonade and slices of cake while jazz played softly from speakers.

When someone tapped on a microphone, everyone looked around to see Professor McLeary. He smiled out over the crowd.

"I would like to congratulate all our graduates, and wish you the very best as you embark on your first steps into the industry. Today, I have the pleasure of welcoming to the stage your Valedictorian, Esther Emami, who has requested to read for you a few verses from the Sons of Martha."

The crowd applauded as Esther stepped up to the stage.

"Thank you, Professor McLeary." She looked out over the crowd and her eyes locked with Ben's. "I would like to ask each of the engineers present to place the ring on their little finger, if they have not, and to raise their hand."

Ben smiled. Each of the new graduates slipped on the ring and raised their hands, pinky fingers extended. In the crowd, many of the parents and mentors did the same, as did the seven wardens.

"The Sons of Mary seldom bother, for they have inherited that good part; But the sons of Martha favor their mother of the careful soul and troubled heart," Esther said. Her eyes stayed locked with Ben's. "And because she lost her temper once, and because she was rude to the Lord her Guest, Her Sons must wait upon Mary's Sons, world without end, reprieve or rest."

He was still in the garden, still hearing the birds singing and the wind in the trees, but part of Ben was far away, picturing the first such ceremony—in a different hall, with a different reading…and with Ginette in attendance, watching her husband's legacy become more than just a name, a story.

He could see Alec's ring in his mind's eye, reforged into the rough-hewn shape of the Iron Ring. Archibald McDougall had presented it to Ginette, and she… What had she done with it? Ben pictured her holding it in her palm before turning to give it to Luc, a boy he pictured as growing tall like his father.

Esther could not possibly be picturing the same event in her mind's eye, but Ben saw the sheen of tears in her eyes as her voice cut through the summer air.

"Raise ye the stone, or cleave the wood to make a path more fair or flat; Lo, it is black already with blood some Son of Martha spilled for that!"

And where had Theodore Cardinal been that day? Had he known what was happening nearby? Ben pictured him staring down at a child who would bear a different name—a mask, to hide their father's shame. But had Cardinal ever been ashamed?

Ben would never know. He only knew that the life Cardinal had experienced, the days in the rocking chair on the porch, the Christmases by the fireplace, was something Alec had never been able to.

"Not as a ladder from earth to Heaven," Esther said, and her voice was softer now, her eyes searching Ben's expression, "not as a witness to any creed, But simple service simply given to his own kind, in their common need."

And what of the others, then? What about Ralph, who had walked away from the project? What of Jean, who had accompanied Ginette when she protested the opening of the bridge? He was not a man who would forget the gift of his own life, Ben thought. He would have remembered Alec, told his children about Alec, and the bridge, and the failures that led to its collapse.

He would have visited Alec's grave, perhaps to lay a rivet there in remembrance.

"And the Sons of Mary smile and are blessed— they know the angels are on their side." Esther was not looking down at the paper; she knew these words by heart. "They know in them is the Grace confessed, and for them are the Mercies multiplied.

"They sit at the Feet—they hear the word—they see how truly the Promise runs.

They have cast their burden upon the Lord, and— the Lord, He lays it on Martha's Sons!"

Esther raised her hand, pinky finger extended, and there was a moment of perfect silence—silence, and promise. Ben broke his eyes away from Esther's at last and let them drift closed for a moment before looking up to the sky, where a monarch butterfly flapped its wings above his head.

EPILOGUE

"**D**ada!" There was the sound of pounding feet and a toddler came around the doorway at high speed.

"Luc." Ben knelt down and laughed when his son slammed into him. "It is so good to see you. But why are you up so late, hmm?"

"That's the new update: he can open his bedroom door now." His wife, Leah, came around the door with a rueful smile, wiping her hands on a dish towel. When Ben stood up with Luc in his arms, she tilted her head for a kiss. "How was the happy hour?"

"Good." Ben hefted Luc against his hip. "Should I take you back to bed, little man?" He laughed when his son shook his head stubbornly.

The boy's eyelids were already drooping, however. He had clearly been keeping himself awake until his father got home, and now he was quickly running out of energy. Content that Luc would soon be asleep, Ben wandered back into the kitchen to see the second surprise of the night: the elder sibling, Alana, focusing with all her five-year-old willpower on mixing a bowl of cookie batter.

"She didn't want to stay in bed if Luc was up," Leah explained with a smile. "So, we decided to make cookies."

"A good choice." Ben came to kiss the top of Alana's head. "Hello."

"Hi, Dada." She didn't look up. Her tiny face was screwed up with concentration.

"So, how is everyone?" Leah leaned against the counter and took a sip from a glass of wine.

"Good." Ben shifted Luc slightly so he could lean as well. "We actually got Tyler to come this time, which was a nice surprise. I didn't think he was going to get back from Dubai in time. He complains a lot about crazy clients, but he's really enjoying himself, honestly. Uh…Kira is working with some car manufacturer on something to do with tires and concrete and…not important."

"Thank you." Leah grinned at him. Over the years, the two of them had learned how much detail the other could absorb about their relative areas of expertise.

"Let's see." Ben considered. "Jamie is still in the same job. They must have offered him a million promotions. He says he prefers drafting to management. Honestly, I can't blame him."

"Yeah, he's a wise man." Leah went to investigate the bowl of cookie dough. "Very good! Should we measure out the cookies, do you think?"

"Yeah." Alanna danced around with glee on her little stool as her mother got out a big spoon and a cookie sheet. "Can I make the cookie balls?"

"Yes." Leah kissed the top of her head and shrugged at Ben behind their daughter's back.

Ben grinned at her. "Uh, who else. Did you ever meet Harry? No? Oh—Esther is being made partner at Klein & Graff. Well, Klein & Graff & Emami, I guess. And she had her first kid just a few months ago, I think. Recently enough that her eyes have those new-parent rings."

"I can't imagine getting a promotion at the same time there was a newborn in the house." Leah chuckled. "Is the baby cute?"

"Kind of."

She raised an eyebrow.

"Okay, he's cute." Ben shrugged and tightened his arms around Luc, who was now soundly asleep. "But not as cute as these two."

Leah came to kiss him on the cheek. "You might be just the littlest bit biased, my love."

"Possibly. Oh, and my mom texted, she and Steve are coming back on the 24th. They wanted to get dinner."

"Sounds good." She leaned over to check on the oven.

"Dada," Alana interrupted.

"Yes?" Ben looked over at her. "You sleepy? Should I take you back to bed?"

"No." She gave him a look she had inherited directly from her mother. "Then I wouldn't get cookies."

"It's hard to argue with that. So, what did you want to say?"

"What's that ring?" Alana pointed to his hand. "The silver one."

"Oh." Ben smiled at her. "I usually keep this at work, but I wore it to happy hour. It's a part of my job. D'you want to hear about it?"

She nodded.

"Okay." Ben leaned sideways a bit awkwardly to scoop her into his other arm. "Oof, you're getting so big! I think you must have had another growth spurt."

She giggled.

Ben headed into the living room, and Leah—after putting the tray of cookies in the oven—followed. She took Luc from Ben's arms and held him close, smiling contentedly, as Ben sat down with Alana on his lap.

"This ring," Ben said seriously, "is for people like Dada, to remind us to be careful. Like when Mama and I tell you to be careful with the lamps."

Alana looked over to one of the tables, recently devoid of a lamp. "Oh," she said, in a small voice.

"Everyone makes mistakes," Ben told her seriously. "Everyone. You, me, Mama, everyone. This ring reminds me to be as careful as I can, and to listen to people who tell me that I might be doing something dangerous—like you listen to me and Mama, and like Luc listens to you."

She nodded.

"But for *us*," Ben said, "for *our* family, it is a very special symbol. Let me tell you a story…"

ACKNOWLEDGEMENTS

First and foremost, I would like to thank Philippa Werner for her help with this novel, and Robyn Miller for her work on the original story.

The premise was decades in the making. From the day my mom posted an article on our fridge reading, "*Verily, I say unto ye, marry not an engineer*", to the time my dad, an engineer, suggested, "Don't go to university, stay at home in the basement and write music", the profession seems to have always influenced me.

Lacking confidence in creative arts as a career, and finding success in mathematics, I enrolled in McMaster's engineering program.

During Frosh Week, my cousin Wes visited with a bottle of Crown Royal and an invitation to a party. I turned him down to study for a math placement test the following morning. The 'test' was in fact a ruse, staged by the Redsuits, who promptly began our initiation into the faculty. Between entertaining events and welcome week parties, they took time to inform us about the Iron Ring, and its historical significance stayed with me ever since.

Passion for movies ultimately drew me into the field, but my engineering degree was forged in Canadian values that would soon come full circle. While filming a movie in North Bay, I had dinner with assistant director David Antoniuk, who discussed the need for great Canadian content. It suddenly dawned on me the history of the Iron Ring is a story that must be shared. I hope you enjoyed it.

Andrew Palmer

Manufactured by Amazon.ca
Bolton, ON

24069617R00143